THE CURSE OF SNAKES

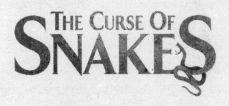

Christopher Fowler

THE CURSE OF SNAKES

HELLION

Andersen Press
London

First published in 2010 by
Andersen Press Ltd.,
20 Vauxhall Bridge Road,
London, SW1V 2SA.
www.andersenpress.co.uk

British Library Cataloguing in Publication Data available

ISBN 978 1 84939 056 9

Typeset by FiSH Books, Enfield, Middlesex
Printed and bound in Great Britain by
CPI Bookmarque, Croydon, CR0 4TD

For Clare and Charlotte

WEDNESDAY

1: Nightwalker

As the yellow moon rose high and the traffic lights changed to red, it came looking for victims.

It walked alone through the town's empty streets. The wind in the chestnut trees dropped away, as if in fear of its approach. It glided silently over the wet pavements and roads. A thousand dark shadows twisted in its wake.

It passed the dead houses one by one. Sometimes it stopped to stare and listen, tilting its head to one side. It paused before a house where the TV flickered in the living room, and waited for a moment, sensing life. All the windows were bolted shut, as if people inside had closed them against the presence of something evil. No one ever saw or heard the creature when it walked, but a few felt it. Parents told their children that there was nothing to be afraid of in the dark, but there was.

Something had been released into the night streets. It moved unnoticed and sucked the life from people. It caused slow painful death, but even those who could sense its presence were too scared to admit it was there.

And now, with quiet deliberation, it was heading for the street where I lived.

A dog barked sharply, then screamed and whimpered, as if it had been hurt.

A cat yowled, but the sound was suddenly cut off.

A dustbin rolled over on its side with a clang.

I was lying on sweat-damp sheets, waiting for the sounds of the city to fade away. The quiet would herald the arrival of a terrible presence. I was expecting it. But I wasn't ready for it.

Before I could think of what to do, the deep silence fell.

It was so thick that nothing could be heard at all. The rustle of leaves, the noise of the traffic, the low hum of city life, everything became muffled and vanished. It was as if a dense layer of snow had suddenly deadened all sound. Or as if the town had suddenly sunk to the bottom of the sea. No movement anywhere – time itself might as well have stopped.

The creature always walked in a pool of stillness.

It was passing by the window of number 13 Torrington Avenue right now, without a whisper. A shadow crossed the streetlight, moving slowly and steadily.

Up on the first floor, in the front bedroom, I pushed the duvet down from my shoulders and listened. After another minute and a half, the normal noises of the street returned, and it was safe again. I heard a distant car alarm. The faint seesawing two-note of an ambulance siren. The wind lifted in the trees. The dog was crying in pain, or was it a fox? I couldn't tell. It was the sound of the city at night, as distinctive as a beating heart.

I sat up in bed and lowered my feet to the floor. I was boiling hot, because I was fully dressed. I pulled my nylon backpack from under the bed and tiptoed to the door. It was dark in the hall, but I could see a light coming from my mother's bedroom. The middle floorboard always creaked, so I carefully walked on either side of it.

I crept down the stairs and into the hall. Stopping before the stained glass windows in the front door, I held out my hand to see if my fingers were shaking. No, they were steady enough. *Let's finish this tonight*, I told myself. *Now. Before it's too late.*

Opening the door, I stepped out into the freezing night and pulled the latch shut behind me, but it still made a noise; it always did. I ran lightly down the garden path and out of the gate, stopping to check inside my backpack. At the brow of the road I could see a swirl of dried leaves, an absent shape, like a hole in the air. I knew the creature had just passed from sight. It was in no hurry, because it was scared of nothing. I was sure I could catch up with it – that wasn't the problem.

The problem was what would happen next.

I knew I might get injured or even die, but I also knew I had to act alone. No one else could help me, because no one would ever believe me in a million years. But I still didn't know what to do.

Ahead I heard the wail of another cat, then a muffled explosion, like the thump of snow sliding from a roof. When I reached the corner, I found Mrs Hill's mean ginger tom lying on the pavement. It had been turned inside out. Its steaming pink guts were hanging on the nearby hedge, like sausages displayed in a butcher's shop window.

I'm dealing with something that can explode a cat, I thought.

My world had always been safe, predictable and pretty boring, but now it had been shaken upside down, and I felt that nothing would ever be truly safe again. There was no going back. There was something out there in the dark that lived to kill – and incredibly, I was the only one who could stop it.

2: Crazy Rainbow
Water Lady

Back at the start of the week my life had been completely normal, or at least as normal as anyone's life in London ever was. My name is Alfred Jai Hellion. I don't like my first name. My dad insisted on the middle name because his father is called Jai. I have a lot of other names, but we'll get to that.

I live with my mother and sister at number 13 Torrington Avenue, in the middle of a terrace. We have windowsills of peeling sky-blue paint, and several slates missing on the roof. We also have the scruffiest front garden in the whole street. My father used to look after it, but when he went away he took the key to the shed with him, so we can't get the hedge trimmer out. People are always sticking cola cans and yellow polystyrene kebab boxes through the spikes of the railings around the garden, and my mum has given up trying to keep it clean.

Opposite our house is a wild piece of parkland known locally as Viper's Green, although the name on the mossy entrance board says 'Torrington Park'. Viper's Green is one of London's curiosities. It should be a popular place for kids to play ball and for families to picnic, and I think in the olden days that's what people did. Instead, it's overlooked and untended, on the way to becoming derelict. The paths are potholed and overgrown. Spiky brambles and weeds have tangled themselves across every route. You couldn't ride a bike through it – not that bikes are allowed in there anyway.

Through the railings I can see stagnant green pools of water where mosquitoes and nettles wait to bite and sting. The water makes the woods smell really bad. The gates had been closed long ago with a rusty padlock and a thick chain, draped around a central iron pole that looked like a massive spear. Mothers tell their children to stay out, but sometimes they still climb over the high railings. There have always been stories of unpleasant things happening to kids who went there at night.

My bedroom overlooks the tallest trees of the park. When I lie in bed and look out of my window, the shifting branches fill my view, blocking the sky; all I can see is the dark green canopy of jagged leaves. When we first moved in, the view didn't bother me. Lately, though, I'd found it disturbing in ways I couldn't explain. The park was closed off years before our family moved here. Nalin, the super-skinny guy running the Am-La Grocery

Store, remembered two men getting out of a council van and padlocking the front gates. Nobody knows why the place was shut. A sign had been put up behind the railing, something about 'council authority', 'illegal trespass' and 'liable for prosecution'. The sign is still there, covered in mould and graffiti, and is completely unreadable. I asked Nalin how long it had been like that, but didn't get much sense out of him. He always talked really fast and chucked tons of information at you, but still didn't answer your questions. Really annoying.

At the end of last term, my friends had started slipping away one by one. Kay, my mate from next door, moved to a place called Cole Bay on the south coast, and my best friend had been taken out and sent to another school for fighting. Kate, my mother, was working long hours in a jewellery shop at the Westfield mall, and was always tired when she came home. My sister, Lucy, spent most of her time at friends' houses, and only came home to get changed or do complicated stuff to her hair.

I wanted a bit of excitement and the chance to make new friends, but in the winter most of the kids in my class only got excited about Arsenal matches, and I wasn't that obsessed with football. I played some fantasy games online, but usually got thrashed. Once I played all day and right through the night, and after that it became boring. Most of the time I felt a bit trapped at home and wanted to leave, but had no money and no way of going anywhere different.

So I waited, and in the meantime I spent my evenings on the net downloading cheats and tips. I like gathering facts. It's different from learning at school, because you're free to choose what interests you. One of the things I learned first was that people fear anything they don't understand.

I was flicking through old hits on YouTube and found 'Crazy Rainbow Water Lady'. She was an American woman who thought that the government was adding something poisonous to her water supply. Her proof of this was the rainbow that glowed around her lawn sprinkler in sunlight. She kept filming it and posting the footage. Somehow, the idea that water droplets refracted light into the colours of the spectrum had zipped right past her. She kept asking, 'What the hell are they doin' to our water supply? What is the government puttin' in it?' She was scared because she couldn't figure out a basic law of science. People scare easily when they can't work something out. I guess I don't scare so easily, because I'm always trying to work out what causes things to happen.

Still, I realized that there were loads of things I didn't understand. There were things that looked impossible and a bit magical because I had no clue how they worked. I've always understood mechanical things, and computers, and how trains operate; I know about plants and how they grow, but girls are a problem because I don't know that many. I figured if they were all like my sister, then it was obvious that their brains worked differently and I would never understand them. The ones who hung around outside the Am-La talked over each other at ninety miles an hour so I had no idea what they were saying. They stood there most nights waiting for someone older to buy them cigarettes, giving off that 'what are you looking at?' thing.

I've always tried to keep an open mind. I felt sure I could discover the world for myself, even if it meant asking questions that made me look like a total spoon. I didn't believe in magic or the supernatural; I trusted science and nature. I've changed a bit since then, of course.

At 4:45pm on the third Monday in October, something happened that eventually made me believe in the impossible. It all started outside the great closed gates of Viper's Green, as I was on my way home from school.

MONDAY

3: Viper's Green

I had walked the route so often that I could get myself home on autopilot. My mum didn't approve of school runs, and said she preferred me to get some exercise, but I knew she was embarrassed about driving her crappy old Vauxhall past the other parents in their SUVs. I made the walk without thinking; out of the school entrance, across the road, left turn, go to the end, don't look in the second-hand videogame store in case you see something you can't afford, another left, cross over, first right onto the High Street, past the Hen Hut and onto Torrington Avenue. But that day it was raining hard. The best protection was to walk underneath the dank branches of the trees in Viper's Green. They spread out above the railings like giant umbrellas. In summer they leaked sinister sticky sap that attracted flies. In the autumn they dropped conkers as hard as golf-balls. In winter the dead branches clattered like old-fashioned football rattles. They never let you forget they're alive.

I was approaching the tall closed gates with their upright centre-spear when I saw a bony, pale boy hunched over at the base of them. He was doing something that made a chunking metallic noise. I slowed down, knowing that I had to get around the guy, but I didn't want to leave the shelter of the trees.

The soaked stranger wasn't wearing a jacket, and it was really cold. He looked up suddenly, suspicion and alarm on his face. He had intense dark eyes, a pointed nose and spiked black hair with longer clumps on top, like he'd cut it himself. He reminded me of a rat that had been fished out of a canal. He looked like the kind of kid who never walked into a shop without working out what to steal. When he took a good look at me he seemed relieved, almost glad to see me. My early warning system went off; I was always careful to avoid anyone who looked like trouble, and this guy had an air of trouble floating all around him like pond-scum. But when I tried to step into the road to go past, he blocked my path.

'What you looking at?'

'Nothing.'

'Give us a hand then. I can do it by myself but it's easier with two.'

'What's easier?'

'It'll only take a second.'

'I don't know.' Whatever the kid was up to, it didn't look legal.

'Then don't. I don't care.'

'What are you doing?' I asked.

'What does it look like?' He was holding a long blue-steel chisel and a hammer. 'I'm trying to get the padlock off. I need a pair of bolt-cutters. You haven't got some, have you?'

'Yes, that's the sort of thing I usually carry around with me.'

'At home is what I mean. You got any at home? You live round here?'

The gate had two locks. One was built into the metalwork, and had already been forced. The other was a padlock at the end of a rusted chain that had been passed back and forth through the railings.

'The council closed the park years ago,' I explained. 'Nobody goes in there. You're not supposed to.' I was suddenly aware of how stuck-up I sounded, and fell silent.

'Yeh, well that would explain the chain, wouldn't it.' The kid's eyes kept darting around. He swore lavishly. 'Keep a lookout for us at least. You can do that, can't you? Just say if someone's coming. That is all you have to do.'

I looked back. The rainswept street was empty. There weren't even any cars. 'No. There's a van in the distance but I think it's turning—'

'Yeh, well don't give me no details or nothing, just

say if it's coming up here. Hold this.' He thrust the handle of the chisel into my hands and pushed the sharp end into the chain links holding the lock. 'Hold it hard otherwise I could take your hand off. They can sew fingers back on, but you don't want to do that because your nerve endings go and you never feel anything again.'

The rat-faced boy raised his hammer and slammed it onto the chisel handle. I felt the vibration in my bones. The hammer was raised a second time, and fell even harder. My fingers were very near the impact point, but I didn't like to take my hand away. One link of the chain cracked open, and the lock fell onto the pavement with a clunk that could probably have been heard across the street. The boy pushed on the gate and slipped through the gap. The hinges whined in pain as the gate opened.

'Well, you coming or what, 'cause I'm gonna shut it again.' He stood waiting with an angry look on his face.

'I'm not going in there.'

'It's just a park. I'm not going to mug you for your phone or nothing.'

'No, I don't think I should.' *That's me*, I caught myself thinking, *Mr Sensible, always saying no to be on the safe side.*

And before I even realized what was happening, the boy had pulled me through into the park and pushed the gate back in place. Perhaps a part of me wanted to be told what to do, or perhaps it was just time to take a chance. Either way, I was in.

Inside, the air smelled even worse. It was thick and earthy with the stench of mildew and toadstools and dead stuff. The dense hawthorn bushes and plane trees masked the sound of traffic from the road. Beneath the heavy cover of hornbeams and oaks it was as dark as night.

'I asked if you live round here,' the rat-faced boy repeated.

'Yes, just over the road. We're really not supposed to be in here.'

'You always do what you're told, then? That must really work for you.'

'No. Of course I don't.'

'Then what's the problem?'

'They put the lock there to keep people out on purpose,' I reasoned. 'Maybe it's dangerous.'

'Look at the place, it's not exactly the Amazon jungle, yeh? How dangerous can it be?' He turned to the pockmarked path and started to walk away. 'The council shuts things all the time. They don't want no one doing nothing they can't control.'

'There are a lot of negatives in that sentence. Wait, where are you going?'

'There's something I'm going to see. Come with me and I'll show you. Or don't, I don't care.'

'You know this place, then?' I hovered, undecided

about what to do. There was still time to get back to the gate. But it was kind of cool to be inside. I'd always wondered about the place.

'I know about it, yeh. Come on or let yourself back out. Look, I really *really* don't care, it's not like I know you or nothing. If you got out of a crashed car and was on fire running down the street in a ball of flame I wouldn't be obligated to put you out 'cause I wouldn't know you, would I, so just make up your mind. And don't start about me having an attitude, 'cause I don't, I just can't be bothered with wasting time.'

'OK, I'm coming.' I ran after the boy, who was already vanishing into the deep green shadows beneath the trees. He had long legs, and was striding ahead. I struggled to keep up. 'So, who are you?' I asked.

'Max.'

'Why do you want to get in here?'

'I want to explore, yeh.'

'What, like an anthropologist?' I was starting to get the feeling that any information I got from Max would have to be pulled out of him with pliers.

'Don't think we're gonna find a missing tribe of North Londoners in here,' he said sarcastically.

'It's something I'd like to study. It's what my father wanted to do, but he ended up going into business. You have to know where you're going and stick with it, he says, or else you get sidetracked.'

'He sounds like a bundle of laughs.'

'My teacher always tells me—'

'Your teachers don't care about you, *actually*, because there'll be another class after you next year and they won't even remember your name no more.'

'That's unfair.'

'Yeh well, life's unfair, get over it, and that's what *my* old man always told me. So help yourself or get walked over.'

'That's not a good attitude.'

'He also told me life is like a shark. Every now and again it swims up silently behind you and takes a bite out of your arse.'

I laughed. See, I came from a long line of people who always did what they were told. Max was exactly the kind of kid I was warned away from. It should have made me turn and leave the park. But there was something about him that made me curious enough to stick around.

'I'm Red Hellion,' I said. It didn't look as if Max was going to bother asking my name, so I volunteered it.

Let me explain about the name. I said I have a lot of others, and it's true.

My uncle Don calls me Squizzer, which is short for Squirrel, because I have one tuft of reddish hair that sticks up in the front like a squirrel's tail.

My mum calls me Alfie-Jai-Hellion whenever I've done something bad, like the time I nearly burned the shed down giving my hamster a Viking funeral.

My dad calls me Cowboy, because when I was small I used to ride the dog.

My granddad Herbert doesn't call me anything because he can never remember my name.

And my sister Lucy calls me The Creature because she's sixteen and spends all her time whispering on her sequin-studded, neon-pink mobile and obviously hates me. My dad's half-Indian (on his mum's side), my mum's half-English, half-Don't Know, my rellies are all sorts from New Zealand to French, but I'm just a Londoner, which can mean anything.

Just to be different, Mr Hassam, my chemistry teacher, calls me Haps, which is short for Hydrated Aluminium Potassium Sulphate, because Hellion sounds like Alum, which is a chemical compound he seems especially fond of. Teachers are always coming up with toss like that because they like to turn everything into a lesson.

So I make sure everyone else calls me Red, shortened from 'Alfred', because it's cooler.

I'm small for my age and look younger than I am. I'm a bit on the puny side but I'm a good cross-country runner. I've no idea what I'm going to do when I leave school. My teachers are still trying to understand who I really am. I told them I'd let them know as soon as I had some idea myself.

'Know why this place is called Viper's Green?' asked Max.

'It's always been called that. But it's really Torrington Park.'

'Nope, other way around. It was Viper's Green for hundreds of years. It got renamed back near the start of the twentieth century, after the last attack.' Max didn't look like the kind of kid who memorized dates.

'Attack? What attack?'

'Some old man was walking across the green and got mugged by a snake. It was in the long grass and he stood on it. It wrapped itself around his leg and bit him over thirty times. His throat swelled up, and then his whole body went black and they had to cut off both his legs without using a whatsit—'

'Anaesthetic.'

'This was all open land. Vipers are native to England. They live in nests, yeh, and there was more of 'em on this spot than anywhere else in the country. They're venomous and can kill you, so I guess he was pretty lucky he got one without much poison in it. If you can call getting your legs sawed off lucky.'

'But they wouldn't be around here now, would they? I mean, we're in the city.'

'You get 'em all over the southern half of England, wherever there's woods, but don't worry – they don't attack unless you like, stand on one or something. They're hard to see on forest floors. They've got zigzag stripes on their backs and an X or V pattern on their heads, so they blend in with leaves and stuff. People think they're bigger than they are, 'cause of the markings. Oh yeh, and they're protected by law – it's illegal to kill them.' He reached into his backpack and threw over a bashed-up paperback: *The Guide To British Snakes & Reptiles.*

'How come you know so much about it? I thought you—'

'What, you thought I was stupid 'cause I don't talk like you?'

'No,' I said, knowing I had just been caught out.

'My old man told me, yeh.'

'So what are you looking for?'

'Tell you when I find it, won't I.'

A huge old oak tree had fallen across the path ahead, and had grown over with sharp briars. Shiny-backed beetles swarmed over its rotted roots. Max hopped up onto the decayed trunk, stamping the thorny branches flat. 'If you don't keep up you'll get left behind. I won't come back for you.'

'How much further is it?' I was sure that Viper's Green wasn't a big park, not like Hampstead Heath or Hyde Park, but the paths all seemed to twist back on themselves.

'It's easy to get lost in here, so the place seems bigger.'

'How do you know that if you've never been inside?'

'My old man worked for the council. He was a builder but he had a lot of different jobs. He was hired to clear the paths, and then they cancelled his work. But not before he saw what was inside.'

'What is inside?'

'Don't know why you keep asking, we're almost there.' Max was virtually invisible in the shadows of the overhanging canopy of leaves.

The passage through the trees became narrower and more overgrown, twisted with mossy tree roots and covered with dripping branches. Even this late in the year, the air was alive with small bugs. They were attracted to the ditches filled with stagnant, iridescent water that lay dotted between the bushes. Viper's Green didn't look like any park I had seen before. It was primitive. A wild piece of deep forest that had somehow survived the centuries as the town grew up around it.

The temperature had dropped. I could hear rain falling heavily on the upper branches of the canopy above my head. My nostrils were filled with the smell of rotting earth. I was wearing new white K–Swiss trainers, but they were now caked with thick brown mud. A wet tangle of earthworms dropped from a fallen tree stump onto the path in front of me. They were knotted together. Whichever direction they pulled in, some of the worms pulled the other way, so the living knot remained in place on the path. It looked like a moving human brain. Max stamped on it as he passed.

I had a problem with things that wriggled and crawled. When I was seven, I had accidentally upturned my cousin's reptile tank, releasing his pet grass snakes all over the bedroom. The memory of the serpents slithering under the bed still made me sweat.

'There, just ahead.' Max was pointing to a dark brick building beyond the path.

'Wait for me.'

The great grey church stood in a clearing at the heart of the park. The railings around it were almost buried in vines and bindweed. Part of the steep roof had fallen in, and several of the brick buttresses had collapsed. Its walls were streaked green. Half its windows were boarded over with sheets of corrugated iron.

We made our way over shattered white stones towards the entrance. 'This was the graveyard,' said Max. 'You're walking over loads of rotting dead bodies. Look at the headstones.'

I stopped to read them as we passed. '*Alice Forthright – In Our Lady's Hands We Place Thee – Born 1894 Died 1918. Edward Beckett O'Malley – For The Light Shineth Bright In Heaven – Born 1867 Died from Influenza 1919.* The great flu epidemic took a lot of people out,' I said.

'What?'

'There was a terrible flu epidemic just after the First World War. It killed millions of people. We covered it in school last year.'

'How far away from here do you live?'

21

'Why?'

'I'm gonna rob your house, why do you think. How far?'

'We're just across the road. My bedroom overlooks this park.'

'And you never been inside it?' Max shook his head in disbelief. 'Can't believe you live opposite and never even broke in here like once. That's so lame. You must be really scared.'

'I'm not scared. It's just a crappy old park.'

We stopped beside the broken railings, where a collapsed sign read:

St Patrick's Catholic Church
Services: 6pm Daily
Sundays: 11:00am & 6:00pm
Parish Priest: Father Christopher Sharpe

A fat brown spider was picking its way over the vicar's name. One of the church's double doors had been smashed apart, and had fallen in. I looked up at the sky between the treetops and saw that the light was beginning to fade. 'It's getting dark. We won't be able to see anything soon. We should come back when it's—'

'Go back then. We're here now.' Max ran into the church, leaving me to follow.

It took my eyes a few moments to adjust. I could make out a handful of overturned and broken pews.

Someone had burned a fire against the wall of the nave, blackening it. There was no altar and no lectern. No candlesticks. No hymn-books. The building had obviously been derelict for years. Only two things reminded me that it had ever been a church: the great height and space of the interior, rising to the dark remains of the roof. Somewhere up there, rain dripped and pigeons rustled. There was a single remaining stained-glass window. It depicted a green-robed figure with raised hands, standing barefoot on a dozen intertwined vipers. A saint blessing serpents. It had no face, though – that part had been smashed.

Max pulled a cheap plastic torch from his backpack and flicked it on, running the beam across the walls. 'Do us a favour, look over here, I'll take the other side.'

'What am I looking for?' I asked.

'Snakes, yeh.' Max called back, throwing me a second torch.

4: Josun

Beneath where the altarpiece had once hung, there was only a large pile of dried oak leaves. It seemed as good a place to start as any. I wasn't about to push my hands into the pile, so I looked around for something to clear it with. A broken ash branch did the trick; soon I'd exposed much of the back wall. That was when I saw them.

'Over here,' I called back. 'I don't know if this is the type you're looking for.'

Max came running over and trained his torch on the site. 'There you go. Nice one.' He knelt down for a better look. They were clearly vipers. The sculpted stone snakes showed their zigzag markings clearly. They were woven together in a wide frieze that ran all the way around the base of the wall. Some bits were blackened and chipped, and pieces were missing, but most of the carvings were intact.

'Why would a church have sculptures of snakes going round the floor?' I asked. 'They've got nothing to do with heaven.'

'You're right. They're symbols of the earth. The church was built here on a spot famous for poisonous snakes. They're reptiles. They crawl on their bellies upon God's earth, so the church shows it's conquered them, yeh. Religion's all about showing who's got the power.'

Max seemed to know a lot more than he was letting on. Clearly he was no respecter of warning signs. I was the opposite of a rebel. At school I worked hard, tried my best to do well in tests, and usually managed to keep out of the weirder feuds that were going on. I made no enemies, but by doing so I didn't make many friends. I wasn't sure if Max was the kind of friend I needed.

'So what do we do now? It's getting dark.' I was aware that the light was fading fast, and didn't fancy climbing through the bramble bushes in darkness. My mate Kay, the one who moved to the seaside, once tried to climb into the park but he was wearing these bright red punk trousers with the legs strapped together, and he fell off the fence and ended up hanging upside down by the strap until I could cut him loose. We never tried again.

Max answered my question by whipping out his mobile phone and firing off a series of shots. He followed the frieze of snakes around the church. Sometimes the pattern broke where the wall had been damaged, but it always started again further on.

'There should be like a centrepiece, a big panel on the floor. Look for a stone where the nave ends, down there, yeh.'

I had fallen naturally into doing what I was told. I moved down the nave searching the cracked, litter-strewn flagstones for the panel, and was absorbed in my task when I ran straight into the dark figure standing in my path. Stepping back in surprise, I looked up at the wild-haired old man before me.

'What the hell are you doing in here?' He reached down and grabbed me by the wrist. His fingernails were ridged and yellow. 'You've got to get out of here before the light goes.'

Suddenly Max was there too, showing the old man a folded piece of paper he had produced from his pocket. 'Let him go, Josun, he's with me. I've got permission to be here.'

'I didn't tell you my name,' said Josun.

'The people in the council office told me all about you, mate.'

Josun squinted hard at the paper, holding it inches from his nose. His mouth hung open, revealing brown teeth. He let my wrist fall. I studied the old man, and noticed that he had a withered arm. One sleeve was thinner than the other. The twisted fingers of his left hand stuck out of it like thin brown fries. He was wearing a filthy blue boiler suit and had leaves stuck in his matted, crazy hair.

After reading the paper, Josun lost interest in us. He thrust the sheet back at Max. 'Don't know why you want to start poking around this place,' he complained. 'Nobody comes here except those little buggers from over the flats. When you get half a dozen kids hanging around in a place like this, you know they're up to no good. Coming here to smoke and drink and spray muck on the walls, and God knows what else.' He looked up at the light fading above the headless stained-glass figure. 'Day's nearly gone. You're not safe here any more. You got to go right now.'

Max fronted it out. 'Why? What's going to happen?'

'Nothing you should know about.'

He wasn't intimidated by the old man's fierce attitude. 'Why did they leave you here? Why didn't you go when they closed the church?'

'I was the caretaker for St Patrick's for thirty-three years, where was I supposed to go? Who else was going to look after the place? The council don't care about it no more. Trying to flog it all off for redevelopment. 'Blocks of luxury flats set in beautiful parkland', that's what it says in the brochure. But where are the graves going to go? There are thousands of bodies under this soil, and they'll all have to be moved somewhere. Half of them died of old diseases, so the ground's filled with poisons. Come on, out of here and fast. You'll need to run, before something comes for you.'

Max stood his ground. 'So they keep you on the site as a caretaker.'

'Without help or equipment, what am I meant to do?' he whined. 'I sit in my shack out the back and wait for the bulldozers.' He started pushing us towards the door.

And you drink, I thought, *judging by your breath*.

'What do you know about the vipers?' Max asked, finally moving aside.

'This is an Irish area,' Josun replied. 'Lots of Catholics here. St Patrick is the patron saint of snakes and snakebites – and the fear of snakes too. The symbol of the serpent marks his territory, see. Not just stone snakes, though, but living serpents.' He looked up. 'The light is almost gone. You must run now, and whatever you do, whatever you hear – you mustn't look back behind you. Do you understand me? Now go!' He gave us a hard shove from the door.

'Oi, that's assault,' said Max.

We set off. Behind us, we heard Josun shouting, 'Run! Run!'

'He's crazy,' I said, breaking into a jog.

'Not crazy,' replied Max. 'He's scared. I'm not running. He can't tell us what to do.'

We were moving into shadows. We heard a strange new sound behind us, or rather, a lack of it. A creeping silence, a falling away of all natural sound that came nearer and nearer, swallowing and smothering and deadening, like being in the vacuum of space. Then, through this, a new noise. A rustling, shushing of cloth.

A soft hissing that grew from one voice to a hundred, as if we were being followed by an entire nest of snakes. Walking snakes. It made no sense.

A feeling of panic settled over both of us. I could feel it creeping up my back. Now we broke into a run. The claw-like branches whipped at us and caught on our clothes.

Whatever it was that walked steadily behind us was closing the gap fast.

We reached the fallen oak. I vaulted onto it, scrambling across the trunk. I reached down and pulled Max up behind me, then we were over and stumbling onwards, plunging towards the exit.

Outside, back in the sickly light of the streetlamps, Max slammed the gate behind us. But the padlock was broken, and couldn't be locked again.

It meant that whatever was inside could now get out.

5 : Psychogeography

'You're stronger than you look,' said Max.

'New trainers,' I explained. 'The soles have got a good grip. So what's going on?' On the pavement outside the park, I bent over with my hands on my thighs, trying to get my breath back. 'You know more than you're letting on. Have you been in there before?'

'No, dum-dum, that's why I had to break the lock off.'

'You're not telling me anything.' Getting information out of Max was still like pulling weeds out of concrete.

'Why should I tell you about it?'

'Why? You're the one who made me go in there! It's not fair, it was me who got you out before—' I didn't know how to finish the sentence.

'Two of us could search the place faster. Keep walking. We need to get out of the sight of the park.

Don't want no one to see.' Max grabbed my arm and pulled me towards the High Street.

'I have an English test tomorrow, and I need to revise.'

'It's like half past five or something, how much revising you have to do?' Max stopped and turned to me. His dark eyes glittered more than the wet streets surrounding us. 'You felt it back there, the deadness. Don't tell me you're not interested in finding out what it was. Spend all your time in your bedroom playing computer games, never see what's outside. You don't want to see nothing, right?'

'I don't know.' I had decided to play it down, because I wasn't sure where this strange new friendship might take me. There was something about Max that removed the safety nets. Being around him made the world a more dangerous place. The feeling was disturbing, but also good.

'Hello, I'm talking to you?'

'Sorry – what?'

'I said let's go over Maccie D's.'

'OK, but it's always full of Prambos.' The local McDonald's was always blocked up with giant military-looking baby buggies.

'I'll tell you what I know when we get there, yeh.'

'I don't understand. Why would you do that? You don't know me. This isn't anything to do with me.'

'Yeh, you're right. I think I'm gonna need some help.' It seemed to take a lot of effort to make him admit this. 'That letter I showed the caretaker? It was permission for my old man to be there, not me. Josun went for it, but I won't be able to use it again. I'm not sure I can do anything more. This place...' He seemed to drift off. 'You know the whole area is connected with poisonous snakes?'

'No. I mean I didn't know.'

'They're everywhere, if you know where to look.'

Max pointed to the brickwork above an old-fashioned barber's shop. At first, I couldn't see anything. Then I realized that a pair of entwined serpents was built into the stonework. We passed a café, the kind that served endless variations of eggs, bacon and chips. A computer print-out menu had been taped to the window. Across the top of it was a fat looping green snake with yellow eyes and a forked tongue.

'Local pub's called the Crown & Thorns, right.' He indicated the sign over the door, which depicted a grass-coloured crown wrapped in briars.

'I can't see any snakes there.'

'A green crown? It's a circle of snakes. The thorns? A sting's like a bite. And a snake don't always look like a snake.'

Now that I was searching for them, I could see that the snake symbols were everywhere.

They bordered the doorway of the Am-La Grocery Store in an angular pattern, and were stitched into the mat outside the charity shop where my mother helped out at weekends. There were even furry green toy snakes in the window of the card shop.

'It's called Psychogeography,' Max explained. 'Yeh, he-knows-a-long-word-shock, get over it. It's when your 'hood gets associated with something like, say, hunting, or horses, or a river, and hundreds of years later you still find signs around. Even though all the buildings have changed, and there aren't any stags or horses or rivers in the area any more.'

'I don't understand—' I was going to say *I don't understand how you know about all this* but something stopped me.

'Are we gonna get burgers or what?'

'I haven't got any cash on me,' I admitted.

'That old one – I'll sort it but next time you pay, right.'

In McDonald's we climbed between the baby buggies to order shakes, and seated ourselves in a battered leather sofa at the back of the shop. Max turned his backpack out on the table. 'I need to download these shots fast,' he explained, checking his mobile. 'Can't see no details without blowing them up.'

'What is it that you're looking for, anyway? Is it like a school project?'

'Yeh, like one, right.' He gave a laugh.

'I just thought—'

'Try not to. I don't go to school no more. I'm fourteen. Well, almost.'

'Come on, they wouldn't let you leave just like that.'

'Special circumstances. Jackie, my mother, she's what they call a functioning alcoholic, right, except she don't function. She's gone a bit Chicken Jalfrezi, know what I mean? I look after her.'

'Can you do that by yourself?'

'How many people does it take to hide a few bottles? Anyway, this woman from Social Services comes around and gives her lectures, *help me to help you*, that kind of toss. I had a home tutor, but it didn't work out. The toughest part with my mum, right, is keeping her from being depressed, 'cause that's when she drinks hardest.'

'How are you going to get a decent job if you don't go to school?'

'Maybe I'll win a game show.' His stare was loaded with sarcasm. 'You want to listen to yourself, yeh. There's a lot of things I'd like to do, but it's not gonna happen, is it? Me, right.'

I looked at Max, with no schooling and a drunk for a mother. My parents were apart, but that was to do with my father's work. They had reached the point of temporary separation without any big arguments. The most difficult person I knew was Lucy. And that was because she had recently stopped being my big sister and had transformed into an alien shopping freak with ever-changing hair who only communicated by texting.

'Why were you looking for the snakes?'

'I'll tell you if you help me do something.'

'I don't know what the big secret is about all this.'

'No, but I do. You can't discuss it with no one.'

'Why not?'

He looked at me as if I was totally stupid. 'Because it ain't exactly legal.'

6 : Crypt

Max drained his cup and set it down. 'Gary – my old man – handled renovations. He helped to restore the old swimming baths at the end of Prince of Wales Road. He repaired and matched the mosaics in there, so you couldn't tell where the original ended and the new stuff began. The council wanted him to work on St Patrick's church, and asked him to make a report on the place. He reckoned the main building could be saved – if the council was prepared to spend the money on a new roof.'

'He couldn't have done a very good job – it's falling in.'

'You heard what Josun said, the council turned down the plan. Gary's idea was to clear the graveyard, cut back the woods and rebuild the church as a kids' centre. You know, so Viper's Green could be used by everyone. When he started digging around the gravestones to see if there was anything valuable knocking around, he found a burial crypt belonging to some famous dead guy. He was convinced the site had to be saved. A hundred years ago there was like, 365 burial grounds listed under London, one for every day of the year, and three-quarters of them haven't been touched.'

'I thought you didn't go to school.'

'This isn't school, it's real life. It's what he told me, yeh. So listen, when Gary submitted the report to the council, they tore it up and fired him. They never wanted the church restored in the first place. They was hoping he'd recommend pulling it down, so they could sell off the land for shops and offices.'

'But that would have meant moving the graves.'

'Exactly. Gary found out there's a local law that don't allow the removal of remains, not without the permission of all the living relatives. Plus, there's risk of these weird old diseases, cholera, plague, the Black Death. He threatened to take them to court, which is like a joke, right, because the only thing my old man knows about the law is when he got done drunk driving. So then he loses his job, and then he goes missing.'

'What do you mean, he just disappeared?'

'He didn't come home no more, what do you think I mean? Look, I'm not stupid, he'd had a fight with Jackie the night before. They was always fighting. She thought he'd walked out on us for good. But that was weeks ago now, and nobody's heard anything from him.'

'Didn't you go to the police?'

'You're joking. My old man never lasted long in any job he had. He was always disappearing like that. Sometimes he'd be gone for weeks without a word. Then one day he'd turn up again and carry on like everything was normal. He and Jackie would have another big fight, then everything would be just as it was before. So no, we didn't go to the law.'

'Did he ever tell you where he went?'

'No, but sometimes he brought me back stuff. Like this.' Max dug in his shirt for the leather cord around his neck, and pulled out something that looked like an ivory arrowhead. 'Check this, it's a shark's tooth with my name on it. Told me he'd got it from a hijacked freighter in the Pacific Ocean, like from pirates, right? They still have pirates there, modern ones. But I mean, for all I know he might have bought it down Chapel Street market from one of his dodgy mates. You can never tell with Gary.'

'Yes, well.' I thought for a moment. 'This still doesn't explain why you're searching for snakes.'

'I'm trying to tell you. Gary was fired, right, but he went back to St Patrick's church. There was something about the place that kept taking him back, I don't know. The night before he disappeared, he come home and sat on the end of my bed. He was in a really screwed mood. He said that something had changed, that he'd found proof.'

'What kind of proof? Proof about what?'

'If I could remember I'd tell you. I keep thinking back to that night. I was half-asleep. I'd walked right across London in the afternoon, I was dog-tired and went to bed early. It felt like I was dreaming. He said he'd found something that would help us. Those were his words. And that he was going to go back to the crypt to get it. Then he took off. By the time I'd got up in the morning he'd gone. No one's seen him since. Jackie started drinking again and lost her job at Morrisons. She'd only had it a week, but going in there every morning with a case of the shakes, they soon had enough of her. I dropped out of school again.'

It struck me that Max had not been able to talk to anyone since his father's disappearance. Maybe it was easier to open up to a stranger. 'The serpents,' I reminded him.

'OK, getting to that. We kept Gary's room as it always was, because Jackie was sure he was going to come back, like he had before. But he didn't. Last weekend I went into his room and went through all his stuff. Jackie screamed at me to stay out but I just wanted to see. And I found something. All the stuff he'd put together on St Patrick's. Here.'

He dug into his backpack and pulled out a thin blue plastic folder. Inside were some photographs of the church grounds, a few pages of handwritten notes and some scrappy pencil sketches: what appeared to be hand-drawn plans of the surrounding graveyard.

'Let me have a look.' I pulled the pages towards me and examined a scribbled note in a margin. 'What is he talking about here? "Impossible to see one and stay alive."'

Max was looking blankly at me.

A plain white business card had been stapled to the file: Simon Davenport, HTD, Tottenham Court Road. On the reverse, an appointment had been arranged. 'Meeting @ 10am. Calcification.'

'What is this? Did you follow it up?'

No answer again. I went back to the technical drawings and read the handwritten notes. 'Snake frieze can be found around the base of the church's interior walls. It leads to the "C". What's a church-type "C"? Chapel? Crypt?' I looked back at Max. 'When we got inside, you didn't know where to look for the snakes, but the instructions are right here.' A thought dawned on me. 'How's your reading?'

Max snatched back the pages and stuffed them in the folder. 'I don't need you, all right? I can do this by myself.'

'If you're dyslexic, it's nothing to be ashamed of. Loads of people are, politicians, film stars, all sorts. It's just the way we're hardwired. I can't do numbers. Look, I'll help, OK? Just give me the pages.'

Max sat sullenly staring at the folder, immobile.

'Give me the damn pages.' I took the folder from Max's hands. 'There might be something here that tells us where he went.' I carefully laid everything out on the coffee table. 'What made you look for snakes?'

'This.' Max pointed to a scribbled sheet. 'It's a rubbing he made at the church.' The charcoal smudge showed a tangled nest of vipers. Their heads were all pointing in the same direction.

I thought for a moment. 'The old caretaker, Josun — why didn't you tell him who you were?'

'I don't want him to know Gary's my old man, do I? Something's happened to him. Gary gets into fights when he's been drinking. Maybe he had a fight with Josun over the work at the church. The caretaker might have killed him. It could have been an accident. No one would ever find the body in there.'

'That's kind of over-dramatic, isn't it?' I said, but I knew Max was right. There are places like Viper's Green all over London, half-derelict parks and green spaces that no one could visit because their gates were locked. Who knew what happened in them?

'Can you think of anything else he said the night he came into your bedroom? There must have been something.'

'I think he must have mentioned the snakes — I think that's where I got the idea about them.'

'Can't you remember anything more than that?'

'It was late and I was knackered. I didn't know it was going to be the last time I ever saw him, did I?'

'He's made a drawing of the grounds. It's not much of a map, no trees or landmarks properly marked, just these boundaries.' A pair of thick lines ran along the top of the picture. 'I guess they're the walls of the church. Those sticking-out bits might be the buttresses.'

'So the big "C" – what does that mark?'

'It has to stand for Crypt. Wouldn't be much of a church without a crypt, would it? He's labelled it for a reason. But I can't tell which way up this is.' I rotated the map. 'I think it must be at the far end of the graveyard, where it's the most overgrown. You honestly reckon Josun might have done away with your father and put him there?'

'I don't know. It's stupid, but I got no other ideas. Gary got into some bad fights. Once, he broke a man's arm in three places. He had a real temper.'

'We should go and talk to the police.'

'No plods. Jackie would freak. Besides, I haven't got proof about anything. They're not going to believe me, are they?'

'Is there some other reason you don't want to go to the law?'

Max didn't have to say anything else. One look at him told me that he had been in trouble before – that he might still be in trouble – and now he could not risk going near a police station.

'All right,' I said finally. 'I don't know what happened back there in the park, it just didn't feel good.

If you know anything else, now's the time to tell me.'

'I don't. I wish I did.'

'OK, we'll have to find out what happened. What do we do first?'

We went outside and stood on the street corner in the falling rain, just by the Am-La Corner Grocery. The shop never shut – maybe Nalin had no home to go to.

I looked over at the swaying trees of the park. 'I won't go back into there by myself. I'll go in daylight. I want to know what else is in there. We can talk to people around here, see if they've seen anything strange near the place.'

'OK. If we split up we can cover the whole street. It won't take long. If you find out anything, call me later.'

'I didn't mean tonight. I've got to revise.'

'No, we need to start now.'

'Why is it so urgent? Your father went missing weeks ago.'

'Don't you get it? Something weird is happening. The caretaker was bricking it – he was so scared he couldn't look at me. And what the hell was it that we weren't allowed to turn around and see?'

'I don't know, maybe he's just crazy and our imagination did the rest.'

'Come on, man, there was something. You sensed it.'

'Yes, I did,' I admitted. 'It's funny, I've been getting a weird feeling about the park for a while now. I mean it never used to bother me before, but lately – I don't

43

know – it's like something has changed inside there. You're right, I can feel it. The sound keeps changing – and the trees, they're moving differently or something.'

'My old man felt it too. Maybe Gary really was going to leave, but he would have called. It's to do with something in there, just behind those railings.'

I looked back into the green dark and my spine prickled.

Max looked at the High Street. 'The stores are still open.'

'All right,' I sighed. 'We start tonight.'

7: Rumours

Our road, Torrington Avenue, eventually leads into the High Street, which has seven shops in it. They include the Am-La Grocery Store, a betting shop with loads of cigarette butts outside, and a fried chicken takeaway called the Hen Hut.

I started with the shops in the order that I came to them. The dry cleaner's proved to be a waste of time, because the staff were new. They were busy pinning pink tickets on clothes in their machine room, which reeked of eye-watering chemicals, and were shouting at each other in Turkish.

Maria Nicolau, the woman who ran the Oxfam Charity Shop, proved better. She was huge and wore a giant flowery smock and a lot of gold jewellery, and always laughed at the end of her sentences, even when she wasn't making a joke.

'Don't you talk to me about Viper's Green, love,'

she said. 'I went to the second-to-last service in St Patrick's, on the Sunday morning, and was never so frightened in all my life. As I came out I heard something shuffling about in those dark woods, something bigger than a fox.'

'Did you see what it was?' I asked.

'No, I didn't dare myself to look, love. I'm not that brave.' She laughed, unable to help herself.

'Thanks for that.' I paused before leaving. *Second-to-last service* made me think. 'Why didn't you go to the very last service of all?'

'I did, love, but Father Christopher didn't turn up. He must have left some time during the afternoon. To my knowledge, nobody ever saw him again. The council locked the place up after that – and the other incidents.'

'What other incidents?'

'Get on now, I've got work to do.' She wouldn't say another word.

Gabriel was coming out of the betting shop, and he was drunk as usual. Nobody knew his last name, or where he lived. It was rumoured that his son had died and his wife had left him, that he'd taken to drink and gone a bit mad. He was always hanging around the High Street, smoking outside the Crown & Thorns with a pint of Guinness, or sitting in the Quality Café with a plate of chips, staring sadly out of the steamed-up window. He always wore grey tracksuit bottoms and a disgusting blue nylon padded jacket that looked like it hadn't been off his back in years.

'Viper's Green – that's 'cause of the snake,' he told me, breathing whisky fumes everywhere. 'There's a big snake that lives in there, under the graves, see. It was once a worm but it fed on the dead bodies, and it became poisonous because all the bodies is riddled with flu germs from the war. And it grew bigger and fatter, but then all the bodies was used up and it had to start taking little boys. It took my Mickey. Never took adults, only boys, 'cause that was all it could fit in its mouth. Sucked all the meat off their bones.'

Gabriel looked as if he was going to cry, but the noise he made turned into a hacking cough. He had an alarming number of badly healed scars across his forehead. He was in the habit of falling down drunk on the way home and cutting himself on the kerb. My mother had warned me to steer clear of him. But I could see he was harmless, even though his breath could strip paint.

It seemed as if no one had ever been asked what they knew about their own neighbourhood. It was like suddenly discovering another side to the people I saw every day on my way to school. They would never have told me these things if I hadn't asked them. But was it all just a bunch of rumours? Nobody seemed to be sure about what had really happened in Viper's Green – they'd just heard stories from other people – except Gabriel, who was obviously making things up.

In the corner grocery store, Nalin put down his handheld game and leaned over his high counter crowded with lottery tickets to answer my questions.

'I know what you gonna ask,' he said. 'Why is it called Am-La an' that.' He spoke so fast that I had trouble understanding him. It was like he'd drunk a dozen coffees and eaten loads of his own chocolate bars. 'See we're open eighteen hours a day so my uncle he was gonna call it AM – PM but I told him PM that's like the afternoon so why don't you call it Early To Late but he say no one knows what's early so it's got to be AM, then we shorten Late to La and get Am-La which don't make no sense.'

'I was going to ask you about the park.'

'Oh.'

'Some people went missing in there? You hear about that?'

'Yeh, I heard about it, them kids that went inside, innit, back around five years ago. It kept happening right until they closed Viper's Green. They went in at night and never come out. About six of them, maybe more I heard, in all. The police hushed it up, didn't they? Weird. See, the Green was always locked up at night and – well, you know how high the railings are, right, you can't climb over them without doing yourself a damage. So the police should have found the kids inside right, but all they found was graves and trees and statues and the old empty church. The kids had disappeared. I mean, completely gone, no sign of them ever leaving. If some nutter interfered with them and then killed them, what did he do with the bodies? See, the park's shaped like a big long triangle, it's bordered on all three sides by them main roads. And there's traffic cameras everywhere, man. The law went through all the footage. They found film of the kids going in, but they never found nothing of them coming back out. Nothing. How weird is that? What did they do, vanish into thin air like some kind of magic trick? That's all I know.'

I had always thought of the High Street as a pretty safe place, but as I talked to the shop owners I began to feel uncomfortable. Everyone had heard stories, but all the information was second-hand. Maybe no one had really seen or heard anything. I couldn't tell if any of the stories were true. But they had to have started some-where.

As I headed home, the wind caught the trees that reached over the railings of Viper's Green. It looked as though the woodlands themselves were trying to climb out. I found myself walking faster than usual.

By the time I reached the corner of Torrington Avenue I was almost running.

8: Algebra

After my father was let go from his job, we moved to a smaller house, the one where we are now. My father left us to work in Delhi, in India, because the money was good and he still had bits of family there. He's supposed to come home to visit for a week every two months, but he doesn't come as often as that.

Kate, my mother, was working late, so I thought I could beat her home – it was stocktaking night at the jewellery shop. But when I opened the front door, I realized she was back. I tried to get straight to my room, but she called me to the kitchen. 'Red, what do you want to eat?' She wasn't a great cook, but she was good at packet stuff. 'Chicken Korma or Beef Ravioli.'

'Can I have an omelette, with maybe some ham and cheese in it? Salt and black pepper, a bit of chilli sauce?'

'Get you, mister gourmet cook. On toast or with chips?'

'No chance of salad then.'

'No, it went off.' She gave me the once-over. 'Where have you been, anyway?'

'Down McDonald's with a mate.'

'You don't like their stuff.' She didn't need to add: *and you haven't got any mates.*

'I didn't have a burger.' I knew we could play this game all night – she was digging for information, and I wasn't giving any out. We'd see who caved in first.

'All right. Just so long as you're behaving yourself. You missed a call from your dad.'

I angrily punched the air and swore. 'Cockermouth.'

'Language!'

'It's a town in Cumbria.' My granddad had taught me to say it instead of accidentally swearing in front of the parents.

'Granddad always says it.'

'Your grandfather is a disgusting old man who once had to go to court for spitting at a security guard in Bluewater shopping centre. You should know better than to follow the example of a man who pulls the filter tips out of cigarettes. Your father sends his love, and there's a package for you in the post. Some software you wanted.'

'Excellent.' I bounded upstairs. Lucy had gone to a friend's house as usual, so I had the floor to myself. Finishing my test revision in good time, mainly because I had already read the set text, I called Max. I wanted to study the notes and drawings in his bag properly.

'Come over,' said Max. 'It's not late.'

'Where do you live?'

'We're on the Torrington Estate, Peabody House, number 72.'

'What are you talking about? Nobody lives there.' The Torrington Estate was the bad estate – the only major no-go area near our house apart from Viper's Green. It had been built in the 1960s, and quickly got a reputation for trouble. Forty years later it was so badly run down that most residents had moved out. Gangs took over for a while, making it unsafe to walk through at night. Finally, the council had shifted the residents block by block, providing them with new homes further out of town, somewhere past Waltham Forest.

'Jackie won't go. We've been here almost since the place was built. There's just one other family that's stayed on.'

'There are gangs on that estate.'

'Nah, they've all been moved on.'

'I've been past the place. There are never any lights working.'

'The power's always going out, and we've got a problem with flooding 'cause the drains is blocked. There's loads of rats. We put down poison.'

I didn't think my mother would mind if I invited Max over, but there were horror stories about the Torrington Estate, and I was interested to see what it was like inside. I figured I could be there in fifteen minutes. 'On my way,' I said, grabbing a jacket.

Torrington Avenue, where I live, is one of a dozen terraced streets that survived the bombs of the Second World War. The streets are sandwiched on either side by two huge council estates. One is bright and modern, and seems OK. The other is the Torrington Estate. It's run-down and flooded, and the kids from Torrington Avenue are meant to stay away from it because it comes under a different postcode, so we run the risk of getting bust up by the few kids who still hang around there.

The estate consists of four shabby grey housing blocks built around a quadrangle of threadbare grass. A maze of waterlogged tunnels and dimly lit staircases connects the blocks. It's hard to imagine that walking here ever felt safe, even when the place was new and busy.

Now, half of the walkway lights were cracked and broken. The other half flickered and buzzed, throwing strange shadows across the stained grey concrete. A long-handled shovel propped against a wall suggested that a gardener had once tended the green, but that must have been a long time ago.

The rows of windows were all in darkness, except for a flat on the far side of the square. I thought how weird it must be to live here, knowing that there were only insects and rats in the flats on either side of you. The dark windows stared down from the balconies like dead eyes.

When I arrived, Max was waiting by the front door. 'Come in quiet,' he said, 'Jackie's almost out. She's hammered the sleepies and washed them down with gin. Once she goes, she'll be dead for a few hours with any luck. I could get a death metal band playing in here without disturbing her.'

We crept along the hall. The flat was clean and freshly painted. Clearly Max had been working hard to keep the place decent. As we passed the half-open door of the lounge, I glimpsed a fat woman in a quilted dressing gown lying on the sofa watching some kind of medical drama. Her head half-turned as we passed, then fell back.

'She spends all day like that,' Max explained. 'Then she complains she can't sleep, wanders around the flat all night. Sometimes she goes down to the quadrangle and sits on one of the benches, just staring into the sky. She cries a lot and lives on crisps. Welcome to the embarrassment that is my life.'

'Is this because of your father?'

'Yeh, but she's always been a bit Loony Tunes. Let's go to my room.'

'Excellent.' I looked around at the Manga characters, superhero models and tech-gadgets that filled the spaces between Max's bed and his desk. 'You got Death-Hammer 4, that's not even out yet. Where did you get all this stuff?'

'I traded it with some of the kids who were leaving the estate. The council moved them to smaller places, so they couldn't take everything. And I nicked some of it, just the small stuff.'

I tried not to look surprised. Max was free to do whatever he wanted and was clearly in charge at home. Some kids were forced to grow up faster than others. It seemed like a good idea at first, but I could see there was a bad side to it. Better to go and live with your grandparents like some of the other kids in class, except you end up using old-fashioned phrases that mark you out as a Nan-Kid.

I got down to business. 'OK, I talked to nearly everyone in the shops opposite the park, and they'd all heard things about missing people and someone bad who lives in the woods, like a molester or something. But no one had really seen anything with their own eyes. Let me have another look at the map of the cemetery. Your father said he was going there, so I guess that's where we start.'

Max had laid out everything on his desk. It was obvious to me now that Gary's drawing of the churchyard marked the site of a crypt – he'd even drawn what appeared to be a nest of snakes in the centre of it, marked with that big letter 'C' – but it didn't make any sense because nothing was in the right place. No matter which way I turned it, I couldn't understand its shape or scale. Finally, I had to set it aside.

Max had transferred the photographs he'd taken on his mobile to his PC. Together, we studied the pictures.

'Check these out,' said Max. 'Most of the snake-heads point in the same direction, but every fifth or sixth one is facing a different way, right.'

'Go back to the first shot, where the frieze starts.' The first panel showed a Celtic cross, a star and what might have been the figure of a saint. Except that this, like the stained-glass window, was also missing its head. 'Can you print these out and join them together?'

'No problem.' We spent the next half-hour cutting and taping the pictures into a single band. Max studied the finished product, puzzled. 'What you thinking?' he asked me.

'That these are a better guide to where the crypt is than your dad's manky drawing. Look, the cross is the church, the star gives the orientation – the North Star is always used on maps so you can tell which way up they are. And the figure of the saint is the stained-glass window, so from this we can get the direction. You ever do algebraic stuff? Where you assign letters different meanings. I think that's what the sculptor of the snakes did.'

'Why do you think that?'

'They're all regularly paced, it's like footsteps. If each viper-head is a single footstep, every time one turns in a different direction, that's where you'd turn. It's kind of a code.'

'Indiana Jones in North London, give it a rest.'

'No. Churches were always putting in stuff like this.

Floors that act like sundials, bricks that measure the days in the year, secret symbols cut into the woodwork of benches, it's true. Then again, maybe it won't lead to anything. But it's worth checking out.'

'You play too many online fantasy games.'

'Yes, I get to read maps quite a lot.'

Max looked sour but was quietly impressed. It gave me an idea about how our friendship might work. I gave Max some geek knowledge, and Max gave me a bit more nerve. That seemed like a fair exchange.

'Is it weird living here?'

'I'm used to it. We'll have to move eventually. Some of the walkways aren't safe. The floors are cracking up. Water comes through. I bought an air rifle to deal with the rats, but the buggers can really shift.'

'Is there anyone else here your age?'

'Yeh,' said Max, having reached a decision. 'Listen. Maybe there's someone I want you to meet.'

It sounded a bit mysterious to me, but I agreed.

9: Emma

I was born in the very centre of London, right in Piccadilly Circus. My mother had been frightened by a taxi as she was crossing the road and had to be helped to a traffic island, where she gave birth to me right on the spot. It was in the papers and everything. I pride myself on the fact that no one can ever be more of a Londoner than me. My dad's mum's from Delhi, my mum's dad – well, nobody knows what happened to him – but me, I'm from Piccadilly Circus, how cool is that? Nothing should surprise me, being a city boy and all, but the Torrington Estate – well, I still don't know how somebody like Emma could come from somewhere like that.

'She and her mum stayed on because of Jackie,' Max explained as we hopped over the flooded sections of the balcony, heading towards the floor below. 'There's only two flats still occupied now. Used to be four hundred families living here. Everyone else has been rehoused. Here.' Max stopped before a red door and knocked on it. 'Their bell don't work. Nothing in their dump flat works.'

The place looked as if it was in darkness. There was no sign that the apartment was inhabited. After a few moments, though, the door was opened. The girl who stood before us was as pale as fog. Straight blonde hair fell about her thin neck; she looked in need of a few hot meals. Her eyes caught my attention; dark and deep, with purple crescents beneath them like bruises, as though she had not slept for weeks. Yet at the same time, there was something about her that was incredibly calm and beautiful, like a lake in morning mist. Once seen, I knew she wouldn't be easily forgotten. She ignored me to study Max, and it was clear that she cared about him. Hardly surprising, as they were from the only two families left here.

'Hey, Maxim, come in.' She stepped back from the door, almost vanishing into the dimness of the hall.

'Emma, who's calling at this hour?' shouted an angry voice. 'It's bloody late to come calling. I don't want callers. Tell them to go away.'

'It's for me, Mum. It's nothing to do with you, incredible as that may seem.' Emma quickly pulled the front door shut behind her, as if she was ashamed of where she lived. 'She's been in one of her crazy moods all day. She keeps moving the furniture around, says there are snakes hiding in the room. She's getting worse. Let's go down to the square.'

A hand slapped against the bedroom window that looked out onto the balcony, making me jump. I looked up and saw Emma's mother in silhouette, her hair as wild as a nest of worms, staring out at us. The other two ignored her. I figured they were used to her theatrical displays.

'This is Red,' said Max. 'He's helping me.'

Emma played with the brown strands of cord tied around her thin wrist while she studied me. Her T-shirt had a picture of a Chinese warrior on it. 'Don't let him pull you too far into his mad little world, Red,' she said. 'He's a danger to know. He'll have you believing all kinds of stuff.'

I laughed uneasily. 'Yes, he's doing that, all right.'

'What's wrong with Diane?' Max asked, nodding back up at Emma's mother.

'What's right with her, more like. She's rowing herself away from the world of sanity, Max. You know all about that.'

'Her mother and my mother were friends,' Max explained. 'Diane and Jackie beat the eviction orders together. There was another woman who we used to call Auntie Iris, right. The three of them locked themselves in their flats and wouldn't move, finally the council left us all alone. Auntie Iris was the first to go nuts. First she went veggie, then she was reading crystals and talking about machines having souls. Divorced Woman Syndrome.'

'That's really sexist, Max.' Emma slapped him on the shoulder.

'The doctors came and put her away somewhere, and then she died.'

'My mum's going that way, too,' said Emma. 'She thinks we'll all go to hell for our sins, unless we start following the exact words in the Bible, like we're all going to be turned into pillars of salt.'

'What do you mean?'

'You know, Lot's wife got turned into a pillar of salt for looking back at the evil city of Sodom. She never used to be so nuts. It's living here that's done it. If she gets any worse I'm going to lock her in her room at night.' She looked at me as if properly noticing me for the first time. 'Has he managed to get inside Viper's Green yet?'

I looked at Max, not sure what to say. Max nodded. 'Yes,' he admitted.

'Be careful. You'll be butt-deep in weirdness before you know it.' Her dark eyes narrowed when she looked at Max, but there was affection in them. 'He wanted to take me in there.'

'You didn't take him up on the offer?'

'I'm not so stupid.'

'Great,' said Max, 'just talk about me like I'm not here.'

'I know about the people who went missing,' said Emma. 'There are probably junkies sleeping in there

61

who'd stab you for your travel card. Max, I have to head back. You know how she gets when she's left alone.'

'You around later?'

'Maybe, if I can swing it. Call my mobie first.'

She was off across the quadrangle to the far side, her pale arms swinging as she walked beneath the broken lights, past the mounds of leaves and the gardener's unloved shovel. A moment later she had run up the stairs and was gone.

'Her mother, my mother and Auntie Iris, what a trio,' said Max, with a bitter laugh. 'Jackie hides bottles of gin in the toilet cistern but she's sad, not mad. Iris drank kitchen cleaner in the hospital and had to have her stomach pumped. The next time she tried, the doctors didn't get to her in time. Now Diane's going the same way, and everyone else has buggered off. It wasn't their fault, it's this place.'

'But you've got something going with Emma. She watches you.'

'She's six months older than me. I don't fancy her or nothing. I kissed her once, but nothing else happened. She's kind of like a sister.'

'She's not like my sister.'

'She and I get each other, that's all. Same screwed-up background. I feel sorry for her. She was treated really bad by the boys on the estate. Can you get some time out of school tomorrow?'

'I've got a double games period after lunch. I'm good at being excused because I tore a tendon in football last year and they think I keep having to get it checked out. Nobody ever wants me on their side anyway.'

'Excellent. I'll meet you outside Viper's Green at one. With the snake map we should be able to find the crypt. Maybe Gary's drawing didn't get the scale right. Come on, Indiana, I'll get you back out of the estate.'

'I can remember the way back.'

'It's better I take you.'

'I thought you said it was safe.'

'Yeh, pretty much, most of the time. But not always when it's dark.'

The inhabitants of number 13 Torrington Avenue suddenly seemed very normal in comparison to the disconnected people living on the derelict estate. The house was familiar and comforting. I could smell sausages and onions frying. My mother was working on her laptop, and I was even pleased to see Lucy.

'Did you have a good sleepover last night?' I asked my sister, patting her on the head as I went to the fridge. Lucy was painting her nails with blue glitter.

'What's wrong with you?' she said, shaking my touch out of her hair. 'Where have you been? We were about to call the child-catcher.'

'You're not the only one with a private life, you know,' I told her.

'Yeh, right, like you can spend more than two hours away from your computer without getting a total withdrawal attack.'

'I'm sorry, my dear, your call did not go through. Please ring back later.'

'I'm surprised you haven't got S.A.D. from never seeing any sunlight.'

'My room is the international nerve centre of a vast underground network. As opposed to resembling the House of Barbie.'

'Mum! Stop The Creature from talking to me like that!'

I took some biscuits and a fizzy water to my room. I ran searches on vipers and the snakes of the British Isles until I was tired, then turned in, but my sleep was disturbed by half-formed thoughts.

I saw Emma, pale and haunted, trapped in shadows, asking for help. Above was her mother, mad-haired, peering desperately out from the window of her locked bedroom. Then I was in corridors of stone, as behind me a faceless figure stepped down from a stained glass window.

The scene settled. Now I was walking through the woods. Something wrapped in long grey-green rags was walking at the edge of my sight, moving in a stately fashion between the trees, keeping pace with me. I wanted to see what it was, but didn't dare to look. I knew it had no need to dart away and hide, because it feared nothing.

If I could just catch a glimpse. I peered through the passing trunks, squinting through shards of light like splinters of ice. I was trying to see inside the gloom, when suddenly it reared up and was right in front of me.

I tried to wake myself up, but the strange visions returned. It was a weird sensation, like being awake, but I must have been dreaming. Except that it wasn't a normal dream this time. It was like I was right there, watching it happen. I was a witness to something terrible, but I could do nothing to stop it.

I sat up in bed and looked straight ahead at the wall, but the dream-thing continued.

I didn't just see things. I could feel them too.

10: The Vision of Gabriel

Gabriel had been drinking more heavily than usual. The landlord at the Crown & Thorns had eventually been forced to push him out of the pub's doors at gone half past eleven so that the staff could lock up. Gabriel knew that the locals all thought he was a drunken layabout. They didn't realize the difficult times he had faced in the last few years.

Late one summer evening, his son Mickey had gone out to play with his mates, and they had dared him to break into Viper's Green. Four boys had climbed over the railings, and only two had come back. The police had questioned his friends but their stories never matched. No charges could be made because the boys were never found. Sergeant Renfield, the arrogant little copper who had taken their statements, had tried to imply it was Gabriel's fault for letting his son hang out on the streets – but how could he have stopped him?

The police said they'd searched the park but found nothing. They told Gabriel that they thought the boys had run away. There had been reports of a kid matching Mickey's description on the south coast, near Folkestone. They tried to suggest that Gabriel had not been a good father.

Since the loss of his son, everything in Gabriel's life had gone wrong. His marriage had broken up, he'd lost his job, he'd got himself into debt. His story had been told in the local paper, which made it worse. Now he was a figure of ridicule, someone all the neighbourhood children made fun of. Whenever he got drunk, he told himself he would move far away, so that he would never have to look at those darkly shifting trees again. But before he could make any proper plans, he would think about his blue-eyed son and start to cry. And he was crying now.

I could see the tears running down his stubbly cheeks.

A full moon had risen high above Nalin's grocery store. Gabriel nearly fell over as he came round the corner. He was drunk and angry. Something had happened to Mickey in Viper's Green, he was sure of it, even if the police didn't believe it had. They said the boy had probably hitched a ride, but why would he? Father and son were as close as peas in a pod. They had loved each other. Gabriel regularly wrote to the papers, but they had stopped running his letters.

He stumbled across the road and swayed to a stop, looking up into the rustling branches. That caretaker, Josun, he knew more than he was letting on, for a start. The police had questioned him but they reckoned he had a foolproof alibi, and had nothing to do with Mickey's disappearance.

He crossed the road to walk beside the park, as if being nearby might somehow provide him with an answer.

The wind suddenly died away, leaving silence. The last car on the High Street turned a corner and was gone. The trees stilled themselves. The rain was still falling, but Gabriel could no longer hear it. All he could hear was his own breathing, like being underwater.

A branch cracked sharply behind him, but the sound was distant and faint. Gabriel was Guinness-drunk, a thick, furry kind of drunkenness that blotted out the senses. But even through this he could hear something coming nearer.

I could hear it coming nearer.

Firm, deliberate footsteps drifting over mud and wet leaves. The hiss of coarse material, as though whatever walked behind him was wearing a sheet or a hospital gown. The temperature was falling. Gabriel could see his breath, feel the goose-pimples rising on his arms. He turned around and peered into the darkness behind the park gates.

The footfalls were closer now. He heard the great gate whine open. And there was a new noise, the hissing of snakes, a great many of them, tongues flickering, writhing over each other, tasting the heavy air.

Part of him wanted to get away, but he knew that if he was ever to discover what had happened to his son, he would have to stay. He would have to turn around and look in the eyes of his boy's attacker. Because whatever was following him had once followed Mickey. He was sure of that.

And so he turned his head, and stared.

I turned my head and stared.

The creature had bare feet. Its arms were by its sides. Gabriel could not take in the details of its appearance, but sensed that they were all wrong somehow. It seemed tall, and was wrapped in long strips of greyish-green cloth that flapped in a silent breeze. The wind enveloped the creature, as though it was moving within a hurricane of its own conjuring.

Gabriel's eyes travelled upwards to the face. When he saw its yellow eyes, he fell back in shock.

Or he would have fallen back, but now his right leg refused to move. It had become rooted to the pavement, almost as if it was becoming a part of the paving stones. He moved, but the leg stayed exactly where it was, as if it had been bound there. He heard the bone crack below his knee-cap. He reached down to touch the meat of his leg, but it was already beginning to harden and crust over. A stinging sensation rippled around his skin, like a million tiny electric shocks. They left behind a deadness.

He could no longer feel the lower half of his body. The numbing sensation was spreading fast.

He had an inkling now of how Mickey had died, and why no one had found him. But the stinging and cracking had crawled up his chest to reach his throat.

It was too late to scream. The spit dried in his mouth. His tongue bulged and hardened into something fat and leathery. His eyes felt like they were on fire. His veins were being blocked with blood that thickened into a gritty soup. He would follow the path of his beloved son, but there was nobody left to miss him.

A van had turned into the High Street, and was heading towards the parade of shops, and the park opposite. Gabriel wanted to call out, to get help from the driver, but it was too late.

The searing fire reached his brain, and as he fell he heard his bones shattering like dry timber. He was unconscious before he hit the pavement. And then, just moments later, he was gone – dragged away into the parklands.

I watched as his body was dragged away into darkness.

Then the vision broke up into pixels, and I was back in my bedroom, sweating and breathing hard.

TUESDAY

11: Snakes!

I had woken up with the duvet tangled up around me.

I tried to get my bearings. I was still in my room. It was Tuesday morning. The rain was coming in under the windowsills and through the back door. There was a smell of damp in Lucy's bedroom that caused her to make threats about leaving home again. My mother tried to wrap me up in a yellow nylon weatherproof hoodie and get me off to school, knowing that I would take it off before I arrived because it looked so uncool.

I passed the gate of Viper's Green and pulled it tightly shut, even though it was no longer lockable. The rain sluiced across the pavement from inside the park, like poison seeking a way of escape. It bubbled and frothed across the drains. The gutters were whitewater. Global warming, Nalin always said, the weather's going to get way more violent from now on.

I fidgeted through the morning's lessons, waiting to

see if my games period would be cancelled. When the rain showed no sign of letting up, the sports master announced that as the pitch was waterlogged, the class could choose between a free activity period in the library or a gym class. With a silent whoop, I packed my bag as the bell went. I knew how easy it was to slip between the choices and not be missed. The teachers really had to get themselves organized, instead of worrying about the length of time that passed between cigarette breaks. I kept good attendance most of the time and didn't skip classes very often. To them I was quiet and invisible, like a flu germ or something.

Max was waiting by the gates of Viper's Green. Even though he had been sheltering under the ancient elms and oaks, he was soaked through again. 'Why don't you ever wear a jacket?' I asked.

'What are you, my mother?' The weather didn't interest Max. 'We need to find the crypt but we've got to avoid running into Josun,' he warned. 'The snake map points out of the front of the church, and his hut is at the back. Plus, the rain should keep him inside. Come on.'

As we slipped through the gates, I felt uncomfortable slivers of dread settling in the pit of my stomach. I couldn't get the image of Gabriel dying out of my head.

Within seconds we were in virtual darkness once more. The woods reeked of rot and decay, of lives long gone. We passed a dead baby crow, blind and featherless, its sightless eyes staring up above a wide yellow beak. Already, worms and insects were burrowing into its carcass. Nothing seemed to live in here except creatures that feasted on the dead. Ahead, fresh branches had fallen across the path, brought down by the weight of water.

'What do you expect to find?' I realized I should probably have asked this earlier. I was already wishing I hadn't agreed to come along. Maybe Emma was right; you got sucked into Max's plans whether you wanted to or not.

'It was the last place my old man visited. Suppose he saw something inside that he shouldn't have seen?'

'What, and you think somebody warned him away?'

'No, Gary's tough as they come. It'd take a lot more than someone waving a fist in his face to make him leave town. I suppose they might have threatened to hurt us – you know, his family, like.' Max made 'family' sound as if it had inverted commas around it, as though he had never considered the word before.

'Maybe he got into a fight and was injured.'

'He'd have found a way to contact me. Something happened in here that changed him, drove him away, I don't know. I got nowhere else to look except in the pub, and I already tried there. He didn't go many other places.' Max turned to look at me strangely. 'Did I miss something?'

'What do you mean?'

'Did something happen? You look – I don't know – like you found out more than you're letting on.'

That was how I felt. I couldn't shake the feeling that the dream about Gabriel hadn't been a dream at all, but some kind of a vision. I didn't give Max an answer. Things were complicated enough without me going weird on him.

We had taken a wrong turn somewhere. Leaves torn loose from last night's rainstorm obscured the path. 'Look through the trees,' I said. 'There's the church. We go this way.'

The undergrowth cleared, and we stepped out into the tangled briars that covered the graveyard. 'That letter you showed Josun, the one granting you permission to come here. Did the council really give it to you?'

'Told you, it was permission for my old man. I can read that much, I'm not a complete doom-brain.'

'I never said you were. Why didn't Josun work out that you're Gary's son?'

'Maybe he did, but I doubt it. Smell his breath? I'm surprised he could even focus long enough to see us. Anyway, Gary was allowed to bring a helper with him, so he probably reckons I'm the helper. Josun's the kind of bloke you wave an official bit of paper under his nose and he backs off. But I don't want him figuring out who I am. I don't think he'd talk to me if he thought I was looking for my old man. Luckily, he's as dumb as a stick.'

The rain had damped down the foliage. We were able to reach the church without making any noise. There was no sign of Josun in the grounds.

Max removed the roll of photographs from his pocket. 'OK, where do we start?'

'The snakes began at the back of the church,' I said, 'beneath where the altar would have hung. Their heads face towards the entrance.' We entered the building and stepped carefully over the cracked flagstones and lengths of burned wood. I checked the frieze. 'OK, ten heads facing forward. That's ten paces. Wait, you've got longer legs than me. Let's split the difference.'

We paced out the steps, silently counting. 'OK, the eleventh snake is facing left.' We took one pace left across the dark flagstones. 'Now seven straight ahead.'

We had reached the vestry exit. 'The next one faces right, and so does the one after that. Then three straight ahead.' As we headed out into the chaotic cemetery, it started to rain with renewed energy. Fat droplets pattered on the leaves above us. The tombstones stuck up through the earth at angles, like broken teeth.

'Show me your dad's drawing again?' I asked. Max dug in his backpack and found it. Together we studied the sketch, trying to keep it dry, turning it this way and that.

'Nope. Doesn't match up to the walls of the church at all. If this was a game, there'd be some kind of clue.'

'Right, sorry for dragging you into real life, no weapons or energy capsules to pick up, no avatars, no boss to take out at the next level. Must be a bit of a jolt for you, reality.'

'Weirdly enough I can tell the difference between games and reality. But if this was a game, we'd keep following the snakes,' I said.

'Fine, let's do it.'

After a few minutes we reached the edge of the cemetery. 'We've still got another chunk of the frieze to use up and we're already outside,' I pointed out. 'Maybe we made a wrong turn somewhere.'

'Who says the crypt has to be inside the cemetery boundaries? We keep going.'

I marked our paces on the photo-roll as we progressed. Now we were deep in the woods once more, pushing our way through thorny bushes that scratched crimson stripes on the backs of our hands. 'This is getting thicker,' I complained. 'It can't be right. We must have made a mistake somewhere.'

'How many more snake-heads?'

'Ten. Seven straight ahead, two left...'

We pushed harder against the bushes, but the branches were so old and strong it was almost impossible to go any further. Max dropped to his knees and started to crawl through the dead leaves. I was forced to follow him. The smell of rotting vegetation was overpowering, as if animals came to die here in the undergrowth.

Hardly any light could penetrate the cover. The knees of our jeans were wet with putrescent mud.

'...and the last one is turned right around, one hundred and eighty degrees so you face back on yourself.'

'OK.' Max manoeuvred himself with difficulty, but managed to turn around in the tight space. 'We could do with a chainsaw in here, or maybe a flamethrower. Now what?'

'I don't know.' I looked up into the dark foliage. 'Keep looking around. See if you can see anything at all that looks like it might—'

Max had frozen. I followed his sightline.

A pair of wide blank eyes was staring back at us through the branches.

12: Finger

Max held his position, but I pushed a step back and fell into the flooded ditch behind me. The branches above us shook and leaves fell, revealing a human head. It appeared to be covered in grey dirt, but the eyes were as yellow and slimy as old pickled onions.

'What the hell—' Max scrambled to his feet and tore back the branches. It was the life-sized statue of a man, but unlike anything either of us had ever seen before. It was incredibly detailed, right down to the stitching on his shirt collar, and in a strange crouching position. It had adopted the kind of pose you'd use if someone was throwing rocks at you; you'd hold your hands high above your head for protection. Max reached up and knocked on the statue's arm.

'What kind of stone is that?' I asked, rising to touch the statue's back. It yielded very slightly and felt thin, like some kind of shell. 'It looks like granite, but the carving is too detailed. It must be some sort of compound.'

'How do you mean?'

'They made us try stone-carving on a field trip to a quarry on the Isle of Wight. It's bloody hard work, and it bruises your hands.' I reached up and snapped off a stone lock of hair. The ends crumbled like grit between my fingers. 'Look at this thing. You can see the individual strands of hair on his head. There's something really wrong about it.'

Max was forced to agree. The crouching statue was really human-looking, a thin-faced man in his early twenties, dressed like a vagrant. The detailing was incredible. His trainers were worn-out retro Converse All-Stars. You could even see the tops of his perfectly carved ankle-socks. But the eyes were the worst part; they were not stone, but soft and sticky to the touch, as if someone had inserted rotting fruit into his eye sockets.

'There's something behind him. I think it's another one.' I pushed back the branches and found a second statue, but this one was smaller and had toppled over into the undergrowth. It had been here longer, because lichen and vines had embedded it into the soft woodland floor. I tore at the weeds wrapping its face. It was a carving of a boy, aged around ten. The figure was curled into a ball, like someone trying to stop themselves from being kicked. This time the eyeballs had rotted away completely. As I tried to lift the statue, a nest of worms rolled out of its left eye socket.

I was reminded of a trip I had taken with my father to the British Museum. There I had seen the figure of a man who had died during the eruption of the volcano at Pompeii. Hot ash had fallen on him as he lay curled on the floor, leaving his shape perfectly preserved in stone. 'This one's a kid,' I called back.

'I wonder how many more there are.'

'There's something really not right about this. We shouldn't be here. Over there, look.'

I pushed on past the stone child and cracked back several branches to reveal a large stone figure. The priest was lying broken in half and partially-buried in the wet mulch of the earth. There was a cross around his neck. The inside of the statue was different from its coating. It may just have been the erosion markings in the stone, but I could swear it had internal organs.

'It's Father Christopher,' said Max. 'I've seen pictures of him. He was always in the local paper.'

We pushed on into the thickest part of the wood, where no light fell, and there, in a freshly crushed patch of scrubland, lay the most disturbing figure of all.

Gabriel – or at least, a stone version of him – was on his hands and shattered knees in the mud, his head turned up to the sky, his mouth open wide in a scream no one had heard except me. He was in the same padded jacket and baggy sweat-pants I had seen him wearing in my vision. Except now they were perfectly reproduced in rock. His eyes were still his own, except that the pupils were as white and hard as peppermints.

'What the hell happened to him?' asked Max, tipping back on his heels. 'What happened to all of them? They're not statues, are they?'

'No, I don't think they are.'

'This ain't for real,' Max muttered to himself. He kicked at Gabriel's left hand, until his little finger snapped off. 'Look.'

Together we examined the severed finger. Inside, beneath the stone casing, was wet red flesh, with a splintered white bone at its centre. 'It's human flesh!'

'Truly gross.' Max carefully wrapped the stone finger and placed it in his pocket.

'They're not statues,' I confirmed. 'Gabriel was dragged here and dumped. That one, the boy, he's one of the kids who went missing, isn't he? It's like their skin went rotten or something and turned to some kind of stone. They must have suffocated inside their own bodies. We should go to the police.'

'Yeh right, like they're gonna believe us.'

'We can bring them here and show them.'

'They was supposed to have searched in here. Shows you how hard they looked.'

'From outside they just appear to be crappy old statues,' I pointed out. 'Except Gabriel. He's fresher, not that he was ever very fresh. Looks like he saw something and just – froze and died.'

'I don't know how you would know that.'

I thought it best not to answer for now.

'We have to find the crypt,' said Max.

'But the map's wrong.'

'It can't be far away. Viper's Green is overgrown but it's not a big park. We've checked the church and the graveyard. We've covered the area nearest the gates.'

'Where else is there?'

'It only leaves the fenced-off section of woodland right at the centre.'

'OK,' I shrugged. It seemed to be my role in life to follow someone stronger. Even in the videogames I played, I was used to being the sidekick and never the hero. But that was something I was about to change.

We headed back to the path and made our way towards the centre of the park, where a fence of ash poles had been erected around a section of wood. The base of the fence was rotten, and had collapsed under the weight of wet nettles and trumpet vines. It was an easy matter to push some of the staves down and climb inside. Councils often protected small sections of woodland, in order to preserve ancient landscape. But in this case, I wondered if there was something more that the council didn't want to be discovered.

'We go in,' said Max.

What else could I do but agree? 'I guess we have to,' I said.

13 : Touch

I checked the earth around the broken fence and found a knot of deep bootprints. 'Someone's been here,' I told Max. 'Not recently, though.' Weeds had burst through the indentations and had grown to maturity over several months.

Getting through the woods proved almost impossible. The route had become more overgrown than ever since Gary had passed this way making his report. It was like a jungle in miniature, a forgotten land in the middle of one of the world's busiest cities. London is like that.

Max pushed ahead, not caring about cuts and scratches. A thin line of blood was dripping from his wrist. 'There's a clearing,' he called back. 'I can see it up ahead.'

I could see it too, a space where the rain fell cleanly, unimpeded by leaf cover. We slipped and climbed across hillocks of reeds, and found ourselves standing before something that could only be the crypt.

'This is *it*?' said Max, disappointed. 'The great crypt of St Patrick? It looks like a drain.'

I think Max was hoping to find a deep vault, lit, perhaps, with rows of burning torches. Instead, he was looking down at a broken slab of blank grey stone about two metres long. It was split into triangular sections. A dog had done a pooh on one corner. It must have been a very large dog.

'Grab the other end of this piece,' Max instructed. Together we lifted out one slab and threw it aside. The second had been removed before, but had become overgrown. It took much longer to remove. Max dropped to his knees and peered inside. 'I can't see anything.'

'Hold on.' The crypt was half-filled with filthy rainwater. An empty, mildewed McDonalds box floated on top of it. I looked down through the dirty brown water. Apart from the other bits of usual London rubbish, plastic drinks bottles and chocolate bar wrappers, the stone casing was completely empty.

'It's a London park,' I reminded him. 'You could hardly have expected to find buried treasure.'

'No,' said Max quietly, 'I just thought there'd be something that—' He fell silent.

You were hoping for something that would explain why your dad disappeared, I thought.

We remained side by side in the falling rain, until we heard the silence.

All sound had drained away in the clearing. No pattering on the leaves, no birds in the branches, no distant thrum of traffic. Nothing. A sinister deafness had taken over the world, the silence of deep seas.

So clear and quiet and still that the sudden new noise startled us both.

It was just at our backs. Behind us in the thick darkness beneath the trees.

There was someone or something coming our way fast. We heard it crashing through the dead branches towards us. Here, the cover of the branches kept the parkland in permanent shadow, and had turned the already cloudy day into night. We scrambled up on our feet and were pushing back against the thorned brambles, past the statues.

The broken stone priest cracked and crumbled beneath our kicking boots, exposing layers of rotten flesh. A sweet, sickly smell filled our nostrils. Beneath the stone crusts were slabs of grey maggot-riddled meat.

We moved faster than ever before, the bushes clawing at our clothes, our skin, back onto the pathway, over the fallen oak and out through the high gates, into the safety of the rainy street.

We didn't stop running until we reached the parade of shops, and carried on walking even then. Finally, we stopped to get our breath back.

'What the hell that was that?' asked Max, panting. He sniffed his clothes. 'Yuck, it smells like I died.'

'I'm not sure I want to know,' I replied. 'Maybe it was some kind of animal. You don't think Josun keeps something locked up in there?' I checked my watch. 'Look, I have to go to Art Club at four-thirty. If I don't turn up I'll get in trouble.' I wiped a smear of mud from my neck, and noticed the bloody cuts on the backs of my hands as I did so. I'd reached a decision. 'I can't do this any more, Max. I want to help you, but I can't, OK.'

'Why would you walk away now?' asked Max. 'We're close to finding out. Don't you want to do that? Aren't you interested?'

'Yes, of course, but this isn't right, it's just so – I mean, they're dead and everything. It feels like we've been digging up bodies.' *And I'm dreaming about the creature that's causing it*, I wanted to add.

'What are you talking about?'

'I don't know, ever since I met you it's like – things are going strange. They've stopped making sense. I'm lying to people about where I am. It's not like me. It feels like something's changing.'

'That's because you were kind of asleep before,' said Max. 'There are things going on in the world that people like you never notice—'

'Wait, people like me? What do you mean? I'm sorry but people with normal lives and parents and homes to go to? People who basically obey the rules and keep themselves to themselves? Not everyone's like you, Max. All that repressed angry stuff because your father walked out and you have to come up with some bullshit story to make it right.'

'Bullshit story? You saw the evidence! Your old man walked out as well.'

'What are you talking about? He's away on business.'

'Yeh, right, for like an entire year. Just because he comes back and goes with you to the IMAX every once in a while doesn't mean you've got the perfect folks. Wake up.' Max went to walk away, but turned back. 'You know what bugs me? There's tons of secret things going on all around you, but you don't care. You're too worried about getting into trouble. Hey, if you want to bury your head in the sand and pretend everything's fine, go ahead. That's what most people do. So go and do it, Red. Have a safe boring life with your super-happy family. I'm better alone, anyway.'

He stormed off along the street, leaving me standing outside Nalin's corner grocery. As Max retreated, I thought I'd be relieved and would start to feel safe again, but instead I just felt ashamed of myself.

Maybe it was true, maybe I was a coward. It was different for Max, living on an abandoned estate with a drunk mother and a bunch of rats for company, but this wasn't how I lived, and I was supposed to apologize for it? The guy had a chip on his shoulder as wide as a football pitch, and that was his problem, no one else's.

Max was in the distance now. Part of me wanted to head after him and shout, 'I can take risks just like you.'

But I couldn't. I stood there and watched as Max turned the corner, and was gone.

I thought of calling my art teacher and making an excuse about why I couldn't make it tonight, but decided it was best not to show up. I could worry about the outcome later. Then I headed back to number 13 Torrington Avenue, threw my filthy jeans in the wash and angrily watched some dumb, loud stuff on TV until it was time for supper.

When the doorbell rang, I thought my mother must have gone out without her keys. But the shape through the glass in the front door wasn't hers. Emma was standing on the step. She looked as if she hadn't slept since I last saw her. She was wearing a black T-shirt printed with a crimson devil's head. It wasn't enough to keep her warm; there were goose-pimples on her pale, bruised arms.

'Are you going to invite me in?' she asked.

'Of course, sorry. Come in.' I led her into the kitchen. 'How did you know where I live?'

'I asked Max.' She had been interested enough to find out my address. 'I was in the High Street getting some shopping for my mother, thought I'd come by.'

It was hard to think of her doing things normal people did, buying groceries, going to the cinema, hanging out at the mall with friends. She didn't seem like the kind of girl who would have a favourite movie, or a TV show she watched regularly. I was sure she had come here for a specific reason. 'What's the matter?' I asked.

Emma went to the window and stood looking out, watching the rain. She was shivering. 'Thought I should probably warn you about Max. I guess you've seen him again.'

I wondered if I should tell the truth. 'Yes,' I said finally.

'I suppose he wanted you to help him find his father.'

'Something like that.'

'Then I have to tell you something. Gary left them. He just got out like he always did, and Max knows it. His father didn't care about them enough to stick around. Max can't handle the idea, so he invents things.'

'You're sure? I don't know – I kind of agree something might have happened to him. I saw proof—'

'What have you really seen, Red? What has he told you? Gary was fired from every job he ever had. He was in debt. He borrowed from everyone. He even took money from his son.' She turned and touched my cheek with the back of her hand. Her fingers were ice cold. 'I've known Max for ever. He's not a bad guy, it's just that this thing with his father has left him a bit screwed up.'

'The way he describes Gary – it's not like that.'

'Well, of course not. I think it's better you don't get involved. What do you know about people like us? Have you ever broken the law? Really broken it? Has your mother ever asked you to shoplift for her?' She studied my face. 'Of course not. We do it all the time. Sometimes we just have to.'

'You can't judge me. You hardly even know me.'

'No, but I know you're different. Not like us. You can tell a lot by looking at someone's eyes.' She was studying me so closely that I had to look away, to stop her seeing that I was embarrassed. 'Some boys are just too – male, you know? They always go on about getting girls, but it's because we basically scare them. You're not that type.'

'So you reckon you know how boys think?'

'Definitely. And don't even think of testing me, because I'll be there way ahead of you.' She checked her watch. 'It'll be getting dark shortly. I have to go.'

'Do you want me to walk you back?'

'No, I'm fine. I walk across the estate by myself all the time. I don't have a choice. My mother won't ever move now. I have to keep her locked in her room and take her meals up to her. I can't trust her in the kitchen by herself. Too many sharp things.'

'At least let me get you a jacket. You're freezing.'

'I'll warm up when I get home.' She looked around. 'This is a nice place. Stay here, Red. Our world isn't so safe.' She walked into the hall. 'But maybe we can meet sometimes – on neutral territory. Halfway between the two.'

'I'd like that.'

'It's OK, I can see myself out.'

It was strange; Emma's visit had been designed to put me off, but instead it had the opposite effect. I wanted to step further into her world and see what she did, where she went, how she coped with her life. I had never met a girl like her before. You couldn't quite tell what she was thinking, or what she might do next. There was something appealing about that.

I felt the spot on my cheek where her fingers had touched, and watched as she went down the path, fading back into the rainy dusk.

14: Contagion

Emma's visit had decided it; I had to do something. I dug out my mobile and made some calls. Then I rang Max. 'Listen, Max, I've got no argument with you, not really. And it's not true; I do care about this stuff, it's just, I don't know, a bit outside of my knowledge.'

Max said nothing in reply, but I could hear him breathing, waiting.

'I remembered the card you showed me. Your dad had arranged an appointment with someone, hadn't he? I looked up the initials: HTD. It's the Hospital for Tropical Diseases. I got the number and tracked him down. This guy Simon Davenport has an office there. He's a specialist in rare illnesses. I mentioned your father, and he's agreed to see us before he goes home tonight. I want you to show him the finger you broke off the statue.'

There was a pause. 'All right,' said Max finally. 'All right. Nice one. You're on. Let's do it.'

The bus dropped us right outside the hospital, a grim Victorian building with darkened grey windows and a rain-streaked entrance. Several sickly old men in dressing gowns stood on the steps having a smoke, like that was going to make them better. Inside, the place was even more depressing. We climbed the stairs and asked the receptionist where we could find Davenport. She directed us to a laboratory at the back of the building. The entire floor reeked of bitter-sweet chemicals. It smelled like someone was boiling frogs in sugar. We reached a door with a sign that read 'Dr S Davenport Epidemiology'.

Simon Davenport was about thirty, and looked like he'd been in some kind of explosion. His hair stuck back from his head as if it had been blasted there with dynamite. He looked definitely mad. He waved a long arm at us. 'Grab a seat. Which one's Max? Yes, you've got your father's eyes. You ought to give them back, ha ha. I've been wondering what happened to him. What have you got for me? I was planning to get off early today, but ended up having to hang around for some lab results. What's so urgent that it can't wait?'

'Why did Gary come to see you?' asked Max.

'He didn't tell you? He was worried,' said Davenport, balancing himself on a high stool. 'I think he thought he'd discovered a new kind of disease. Some of the cemeteries of London contain people who died of unusual illnesses. Modern medicine has wiped out many

93

of these, but there are still some we can't cure, like various strains of the plague. In the old days, people used to refer to epidemics as "visitations". They thought disease was carried by putrid smells.'

'If that's the case anyone who's ever walked past your office would be dead,' said Max.

'Yes, it hums a bit out there, doesn't it?' Davenport agreed. 'Your father was working near a graveyard, wasn't he?'

'Yeh.'

'Well, he thought some of the people in the graveyard might have died of an unknown illness. Certain incurable diseases can continue to survive in a dead body, you know, particularly if it was buried in a strong, airtight oak or lead coffin. Sometimes graveyards have to be moved, and when we take out the coffins, we have to use workers from particular parts of Eastern Europe.'

'Why?'

'Because we Westerners could catch these forgotten illnesses, but there are people born near the Russian border who have a natural immunity to them. So they can move the coffins safely. Your father had apparently been in contact with water from a crypt that was very old, and he was worried that he might have become infected by something that still lived on in it. He got in touch with the hospital, and they passed him onto me. So I ran a few tests on him, but he never came back for the results.'

'He went missing,' said Max. 'Do you think he's become sick? Maybe he came into contact with a rare disease?'

'No, that's the strange thing. His tests all came back negative. There was absolutely nothing wrong with him. He had some red sores on the palms of his hands, but they were just a form of eczema. A rare one, admittedly, but that's all it was.'

I looked at Max. We were both thinking the same: that Max's father had also found the strange statues, and wanted to know what had happened to the victims. So he had come to see the specialist, to find out if they were suffering from a disease.

'I've been everywhere Gary went before he came to see you,' Max explained, 'and I found this.' He dug in his pocket and produced the paper-wrapped stone finger.

'Whoa, you think you've found something that's infectious?' asked Davenport. 'You can't just come in here and dump—'

'I didn't say it was carrying a disease. Maybe Gary found something like it as well, and that's why he came to see you, I don't know. I just want your opinion, all right.'

Davenport snapped a pair of clear plastic gloves from the roll on his desk, and carefully turned over the finger. 'If this is from a piece of statuary, I have to tell you stone doesn't absorb germs as easily as living tissue. We could run microscopic analysis on it, but it won't reveal as much as—'

When he saw inside it, he froze. 'Well, look at that.' Davenport placed the finger under an illuminated magnifying glass.

I craned forward to try and see what the biologist was looking at.

'This is a digit from a human being. It's undergone necrosis – cellular death – and calcification. That means it's turned to stone. Things do, of course. Sand will turn to rock if crushed for long enough, and coal becomes diamonds. But the process normally takes an incredibly long time, and this is relatively fresh. The outer epidermis looks as if it's been subjected to electromagnetic radiation, but with the structure of a carcinogen-inducing ionizer.'

'What does that mean in regular English?' asked Max.

Davenport sat back and tried to think of the best way to explain. 'Radiation damages the chemical bonds in your body, OK? I could tell you all about low-energy photons, but it's hard to communicate in simple terms. When you go to the beach and get a suntan, there's a chemical change in your skin that darkens it. This is the same idea, but a lot more serious. The change goes much deeper. It's like the skin has dried, then burned and rotted. Look at the centre; the bone has started to change as well. If the man this finger came from had been subjected to the same level of radiation for any longer, the whole of his body would have become calcified in this way. It must have been a terrible, painful death, a bit like being put in a microwave. His skin thickened so quickly that he must have suffocated. Every organ within him would have grown heavier, denser until he was crushed from inside. Liquid parts would take longer to harden, I imagine.'

That was why the eyes were still sometimes jellified, I thought. 'What you're saying is this man turned to stone.'

'No – no.' Davenport ran his fingers through his hair, looking madder than ever. 'There's no process in the known world that can quickly turn a man to stone.'

'Maybe this isn't in the known world,' I said.

'We have to go there. I have to see the body this finger came from. Where did you find it?'

'There are others in the same place.'

'There could be a radiation leak of some kind. I can't think what else it might be. Your father may well have been right after all. Tell me exactly where this place is.'

'No, but we can get you there.'

'It could be dangerous without the proper equipment. I can't take that risk. You should leave this to the experts.'

'Then we won't be able to take you,' said Max flatly. He swung his backpack onto his shoulder and tapped me. 'Come on, let's get out of here.'

'No, I'll have to make a full report,' Davenport called after us. 'Don't you understand? Whatever you've found – it could be something we've never seen before, some process that's been lost for years, or something entirely new. That means we don't know what it could do to you. It could be fatal. It could spread.'

'Fine, whatever.' Max continued, heading for the door.

'Wait, where are you going?'

'We'll be in touch, yeh,' said Max. 'Don't wait up or anything.'

15: Calcification

As we headed off along the traffic chaos of Euston Road, it was me taking the lead for once. 'Why wouldn't you let him help us?' I wanted to know.

'Because he'll bring in medics and cops and we'll be shut out because we're just members of the public, and we'll never find out what happened.'

I knew he was right. 'I've got an idea what this is about,' I told him, 'but you're never going to believe me. No one will.'

'Well, come on then.'

'We need to run a search. You ever use the library up by the bus garage?'

'Yeh, I'm in it all the time. Like I ever read books. I use Gary's old PC but it runs slow now.'

'We could go to my house and use my computer, it's probably faster. Or we could do this the old way. I have a card for the public library.'

'Oh, *man*. Don't do this to me.'

'Listen, they've got some reference books there that contain stuff I've never seen scanned in on the internet, and the woman who runs the place lets me search their rare books section, which isn't supposed to be used by minors. I don't want you ripping any pages out, though, because she trusts me, OK?'

'Yeh, OK, whatever. Let's get it over.'

'I didn't fit the pieces together until Davenport talked about the man turning to stone.'

'Just tell me.'

'Wait until I can find proof.'

The library was an old building that smelled of wet wood and floor polish. An elderly lady sat behind the counter by the door, dozing. She was wearing bright blue eye-shadow and red lipstick, and looked like a sleepy clown. Behind her, rainwater was dripping into a bucket. The place was almost empty.

'That's the head librarian,' I explained. 'She likes to mess up my hair so I have to stay out of reach. Hi, Mrs Rainey.' I made her jump. She suddenly sat upright, touched her own hair back in place and adjusted her glasses to get a proper look at me.

'Oh, it's you, Red. It's a slow afternoon. The radiators are on full and they make me tired. What are you after?'

'The reference section, Greek myths.'

'Well, you've been there before, I'm sure you remember where to go. Is this a friend?'

'Yeh, sort of.' I nodded to Max.

'You know how to use the scanner, don't you? I won't charge you for copies.'

'See?' I whispered. 'She *really* likes me.'

'She's a little old for you, don't you think? I mean, she must have been born in about five million years BC.'

The last customer was leaving. We had the place to ourselves. 'There are some seriously strange books just sitting here for anyone to find,' I said, setting off among the stacks to find a particular shelf. 'Nobody takes them out any more.'

'It smells weird in here. What are we looking for?'

'This is it. Damn, top shelf, can't reach. Push those over.' I pointed to an old-fashioned set of wooden steps on wheels. Max lined them against the shelf, and I climbed up. I removed several books and carried them over to the nearest table.

'What do you know about Greek mythology?' I asked.

'I saw the Disney movie about Hercules. Sucked.'

'OK.' I searched the biggest book, finally turning it around so we could both see. 'There's something in Viper's Green that can turn people into living stone. You agree with that?'

'I guess so.'

'You felt it walking behind us.'

'I don't know what it was – but yeh, that's what it

felt like. Some kind of animal, definitely not human, but somehow invisible, 'cause I couldn't see it.'

'No, you could have seen it – you just didn't want to.'

'What, you trying to say I was scared or something?'

'No, I'm saying that neither of us wanted to see it, because somehow we sensed what might have happened if we had caught sight of it. It gave off a warning somehow – like the weird silence that happens whenever it's around.'

'I don't understand. What are you getting at? If there really was someone who came out of the crypt, and he was after us—'

'Who said it was a he?'

Max looked at me blankly.

I read aloud. *'Medusa, the Greek myth of the crone Goddess in her most terrifying aspect. According to ancient legend Medusa was the "most horrific woman in the world". A creature cursed with snakes for hair, who inflicted the most terrible cruelty on all men . . .'*

'Oh, come *on*—'

'And here she is. Take a look.' I held open the page.

The painting in it showed a woman with green-tinged scaly skin, a dripping forked tongue, and dozens of small patterned snakes sprouting through the skin of her head in place of hair. The whites of her eyes were a deep sea green at the edges. The teeth in her lower jaw were long transparent spines that looked like the ones I had seen on footage of deep sea fish.

'She is one seriously ugly mother,' marvelled Max.

'She can only close her mouth because there are two little holes in her upper lip, see, where the razor-teeth go. She came from the sea, and was once the most beautiful of three sisters. The other two were goddesses, but Medusa was an ordinary mortal. Poseidon, the old king of the oceans, declared his love for her in the temple of Athena and seduced her.'

'What, he had a go on her? Gross.'

'But she didn't look like this then, that's what I'm saying. She was incredibly sexy and beautiful.'

'So what happened?'

'It was a big mistake, because Medusa got pregnant. Athena, Poseidon's wife, was watching and went bananas. She zapped Medusa, turning her into a creature called a Gorgon. At night when the moon is at its fullest, she changes from a human into a monster. Her teeth are transformed into these spines, her tongue blackens and stretches, her hands become long claws and her hair sprouts deadly serpents. But the best part is this; her gaze turns men to stone so that no one living may ever look on her.'

'Snakes and stone people. I guess it kind of fits, but—'

'Medusa can also be beautiful and seductive. But as the Gorgon, she wants to bring death to all men.'

'A bit like having a secret identity.'

'I guess so. Even Poseidon was scared of her. The

only way to stop the creature is to behead it. The problem is, how do you behead a thing you can't look at without turning to stone?'

'I s'pose you realize how totally crap this sounds? I mean, this is a Greek legend, right? Thousands of years old. Like a fairy tale or something. Not real, not in a London park surrounded by vans and old dears doing their shopping at Sainsbury's, and not in the twenty-first century.'

I turned the dusty pages. 'I don't know, there's a whole lot more about her here. She lives in a crypt or temple, and must return home each night after making her kill. She only kills males. She's taking revenge, because Poseidon was never punished. It's like there was this thing I saw on the internet, a thirteen-year-old girl in Somalia, in Africa, and she was attacked by a bloke who fancied her, and for that she was sentenced to be stoned to death. They put her in a hole, buried her up to her neck, and threw rocks at her until she was dead. And the guy was just let off. Medusa suffered too, but she can take her revenge on men.'

'What happened to her?'

'She killed every great soldier sent to fight her. Finally, a warrior called Perseus chopped off her head by looking at her reflection in his shield, which acted like a mirror. He got a special spear from three old women called the *Graeae*, who only had one eye and one tooth between them, which they all had to share. They were the only ones who knew how to kill the Gorgon.'

'Weird-o-rama.'

'I think your dad was checking out the graveyard and opened the crypt. In doing that, he accidentally released the Gorgon, who had somehow got in there.'

'You should be sprinkled over an ice cream, mate, because you're nuts.'

'Then how else can you explain what's been happening?'

'You reckon my old man let out a woman who's several thousand years old – oh, and missing her head, by the way, because she had it *hacked off*, and then she turned him to stone with one look and attacks anyone else who happens to be passing through Viper's Green?'

'Think about the name, Max. I don't know how she's still alive but maybe she's always been there, and people have always known about her. That's why there were snakes in the area. And it's a full moon. The moon in this phase lasts four days. I bet if we checked when all those people went missing, their dates would all match up to the times of the full moon. Think of it, a lethal creature that operates like a werewolf, turning from a normal person into a monster.'

'You'd love that, wouldn't you? It would be just like one of your dumb-ass computer games.'

'Wait, you're the one who started all this, you're the one who involved me, remember?' I said angrily. 'At least my life made sense until I met you. Now I can't even walk down the street without wondering who knows about this, and what's walking behind me, waiting for me to turn around.'

'That's not fair. I'm not the cause of this.'

'It's just you, Max. You're an agent of chaos. Not a good thing to be, by the way.'

'Yeh, well if I want to be insulted I can get that at home – I don't need you to handle it.'

'Everything OK back there, boys?' called the chief librarian.

'Fine, Mrs Rainey.' I lowered my voice. 'There's a full moon until Thursday. If there's another attack tonight, you'll know all this is true.'

'How was the Gorgon in the park with us when it wasn't even dark?'

'But it was. Don't you get it? It's always dark near the church because of all the trees.'

'You're not right in the head, that's the only thing I know. Books! They do my head in. I have to get out of here.'

'Good,' I snapped. 'Go, but if anything bad happens, it will be your fault. You're the one who broke the lock off the gate to Viper's Green. You're the one who let out the Gorgon.'

Max turned on me. 'You're crazy, you know that? Even setting aside the idea that some crappy B-movie monster legend could actually be based on fact, what the hell was a Gorgon doing in a London park, eh? What, did it decide to take an easyJet vacation from ancient

Greece or something? OK, we saw what we saw, but there has to be another explanation.' Max slapped the side of his head.

'Yes, and you have to accept that your father may be dead.'

'Great. Hey, thanks for that. I'm going out for a smoke. You can do whatever the hell you want to do.'

Max turned on his heel and stormed out of the library. When I came out he had gone, so I caught a bus home and went up to my room. I lay down on my bed and stared at the ceiling, thinking. I didn't mean to fall asleep, but couldn't help it.

At first there were no dreams. I guess the vision began some hours later. It was just like last time – but even more vivid, like I was right there and unable to stop the horrific events unfolding.

I opened my eyes wide but I could still see it.

16: The Vision of Nalin

The rainclouds cleared the yellow moon, but no moonlight fell on the High Street, where fierce neon signs shone out in the night. The Hen Hut and the Crown & Thorns were still lit up, but the Am-La Grocery lights flickered out as Nalin closed early.

Nalin looked dog-tired. I could see that he hadn't sold half of the vegetables he kept in boxes along the pavement, even though they were grown locally and better than those in the supermarket. He bent and stretched. His arms and knees ached. He was only nineteen years old but by the end of the week he told me he always felt at least fifty. There were no customers around, so he'd decided to close up. He pulled down the steel shutter with a bang and locked it, knowing that he would be back in a few hours' time to open up again.

He rose and stretched his back again. Now there was a new development – I could hear what he was thinking.

Maybe I should start playing football again. Would that get rid of the ache? Man, how could I get this out of shape so quickly? His thoughts were as clear as if he was speaking aloud. He looked around. It had just gone 10:00pm and the street was deserted – there wasn't anything here to amuse kids, but that didn't usually stop some of the gangs from hanging around until past midnight.

Nalin was thinking that when he had kids, he wouldn't let them stay up after half ten. He knew that when they got bored, they got into trouble. Time for a fag, he thought. He still lived at home, and his parents wouldn't let him smoke in the house.

Opposite, the dark trees in Viper's Green shifted and rustled. The deep crevices between the boughs formed black shapes, as though animals were moving around, watching the street below.

Nalin had never really thought about the park before. It had always been there. He and his brothers had been born in the surrounding roads. Now, though, it seemed different – there was a strange smell, wild and earthy, and a constant noise, like the hiss of a badly tuned radio – and the gate, which had been chained and locked for the last few years, was whining on its hinges like a crying baby.

The cigarette tasted like ashes and dirt. He ground it out, feeling faintly sick. He was about to set off along the High Street when the gate to the park banged harder, and the wind rose about him as something –

some *thing* – crossed the empty road, bringing with it a tornado of litter and dead leaves.

The skin on his arms prickled. There was someone walking behind him, he was sure. He could feel them gaining ground, getting closer every second. Nothing to be afraid of; he had faced plenty of gang members in London, he knew how to handle himself, so what was happening? Suddenly he was filled with irrational panic, and started to jog.

On, past the rest of the shops, past the point where he should have turned into his road, towards the railway line. No matter how fast he ran, the thing behind him moved closer. He wasn't thinking now, just acting on instinct, and somehow he knew that he did not dare to turn around and look at it.

Crash – up over the bonnet of a white van that had turned the corner too fast, the driver swearing at him – and on he went, up the steps to the footbridge, praying he could outrun the thing that had chosen to stalk him.

His trainers slipped on a wet page of the *Sun* stuck to one of the steps, and he fell, cracking his knee against the steel edge of the staircase. Then he was back on his feet and hitting the cross-bridge over the railway track.

But by now the creature was close enough to touch his back. It scratched at him, claw-cuts appearing in his T-shirt, slashing at his shoulder blades, and suddenly I knew he couldn't make it to the other side. I wanted to call out and warn him but he wouldn't be able to hear me. The thing would be upon him in the next few seconds.

There was only one course of action left. Shoving his right foot against the steel side of the bridge and jumping hard, he went up and over it, dropping and swinging on the railing.

I guess he hoped that the creature would move on, across the bridge and down the other staircase. But instead it stopped right in the middle, above him, and looked down over the edge.

There was a train coming – I could hear the rails pinging below. Nalin needed to pull himself back up, but his pursuer was waiting for him.

The creature was curious. It stared steadily at Nalin, willing him to look up, wondering what he would do. His heart thudding in his chest, Nalin looked straight ahead at the wall and gripped the top railing as hard as he could.

But slowly, surely, he knew he had to stare into the eyes of the thing that was hunting him. If he didn't, it would never go away. He could already feel his grip on the rail starting to loosen. He didn't know how long he had left before he would lose the power to pull himself back up.

The track was too far below to drop onto – ten metres at least – and besides, there was a fast train approaching. The station here was small and mostly deserted. Only one train in three ever stopped.

Armed with patience and curiosity, the creature watched and waited for him.

Don't look up, I yelled. *Don't do it!*

And Nalin looked up.

He saw a tall figure in fluttering ragged robes of green and grey. Its arms rested by its sides. They were lightly scaled and pale green. The jaw hung open, the long white spines of its teeth jutting out. The hair writhed and twisted, the slim emerald snakes snapping at each other, as though they were overcrowded on its skull. Then I saw its eyes, oddly flat and far apart, staring at Nalin as if trying to understand what was inside him. It seemed to me that the creature was in pain; the twisting snakes had sprouted through the skin of its head, leaving it split and sore.

When Nalin looked into the yellow-green eyes, it was as if the rest of the world ceased to exist. And as its gaze settled on him, the snakes all turned to look at him too. He was being stared at by a hundred pairs of eyes.

The moment Nalin stared at the creature he felt the change. Something began to heat up inside him, like radiation or a terrible virus, a sick, burning feeling that filled him with terror.

The train was almost at the bridge. It raced and thundered below. Nalin felt his hands changing. The skin dried, blackened, rotted and cracked, and finally split open. His legs grew heavier by the second. Whatever the thing had done to him, the poison was spreading fast throughout his body. His stomach was stretching as the air inside it expanded. He felt as if he might explode.

In a great rush of wind, the train hammered past beneath his feet. As he looked down, Nalin saw with horror that he was turning to a kind of stone. He kicked back and forth, trying to shake the sickness from his body. One heavy, hardened trainer came off and fell, shattering into dust against the passing carriages below.

The Gorgon stood watching, quite still, its head tipped on one side. It wanted to observe and understand.

Nalin could no longer support his own weight. He stared at the fingers of his right hand, appalled, as they splintered apart and broke off. He was suspended by his left hand now. But his legs were stone, and the creaking, crunching, cracking sensation had spread to his chest and up his neck. He weighed so much that the railing was starting to buckle.

With a sharp snap, his left hand split open at the wrist and came apart, the tendons stretching like red strings. There was nothing to support him any more.

With a scream he fell back into the night, down into the rushing carriages, and was smashed into a thousand pieces beneath the rushing steel wheels of the 22:17 express.

WEDNESDAY

17: The Archive

I awoke in a worse sweat than before. My hands were shaking violently. I went straight to my computer and started to run searches and make notes. I couldn't believe that Nalin was dead. I wanted to know what was happening to me. It seemed as if something inside me was opening, some new sense created by the bizarre events of the last few days.

I was wired and tired. I checked the time; gone midnight. Wednesday already. My sister was staying at a friend's house and my mother had gone to bed, so I could work as late as I liked. I wanted to go round and check on the Am-La Grocery Store, to peer over the railway bridge and search for Nalin's smashed body, but I was horribly sure that I wouldn't find it there.

I drank two Red Bulls and ate an entire packet of milk chocolate digestives to keep myself awake. If this was really connected to the cycle of the moon it meant two more nights, two more slaughters. Then the whole process would start all over again next month.

Something had to be done, but how could you walk into a police station and tell them a story as mad as this? With a sinking feeling in the pit of my stomach, I knew that the job would fall to me and Max.

By 2:15am I had gathered together stacks of information, but I still had no answer. It was clear that the solution lay in the ancient past, but I needed a way forward. A course of action. What could we really do? We didn't have enough knowledge to fight back.

That was when I stumbled across the site.

The London Metropolitan Archive in Clerkenwell.

The screen said it held all the documents connected to the city of London – everything. Surely, they would have a history of Viper's Green. The bad news was that not all of their documents were available online. I knew I would have to go there as soon as it opened, which meant cutting school. Luckily I had an unused note for an optician's appointment and would only be missing an ICT class with a dopey supply teacher.

Removing my close-up glasses and rubbing my knackered eyes, I fell back to sleep fully dressed to the sound of the falling rain, and didn't wake up until daylight. This time, I didn't dream at all.

Incredibly, it was still raining at 9:00am. The endless downpour felt like some kind of sign. The London Metropolitan Archive was housed in such an ordinary building that it was almost invisible. You could have walked past it a hundred times without ever wondering what it was. It was opposite a park, but one with skateboard areas and clipped hedges, open, modern and safe.

I tried raising Max on his mobile, but it was switched off; he'd probably not been topping up. I had no choice but to go alone.

The young woman seated at the red plastic desk was helpful. She directed me to the shelves of folders where the indexes were kept – lists of everything they had. These were divided into documents, maps and photographs. I found Viper's Green easily, but the park's plans hadn't been transferred to digital files. So I filled out a slip of paper, handed it in and waited for the maps to be delivered to my table.

The volume that arrived was about three feet long. I could hardly lift it, and it smelled disgusting. Rot had set into the red leather binding. I raised the vast cover, trying not to damage it, and soon found what I was looking for. The first map of Viper's Green, drawn in ink in the year 1537. It had been bigger then; one corner had since been lopped off to build the road at the top of the High Street.

I adjusted my glasses and leaned closer. Dirt from the book was staining my hands, as if history itself was rubbing off on me. There were some scribbled notes along the bottom of the map, written at a later date. One said; 'Site of the Libyan Reliquary.'

OK, I thought, *fine, I can do this. But I need internet access now.*

The archive's only spare computer was like something from the stone age. Its keyboard was covered in dirt and bits of people's lunch. I Googled the reference and it said that a reliquary was a place where they put valuable objects. Next I tried Libya, which was a country that had once been occupied by the Greeks, and was the home of the Gorgon herself.

I went back into the archive and made more notes. In 1918 an English explorer had returned from Libya with several rare Greek objects, including something called the *Gorgoneion*, a stone pot carved with the head of the Gorgon. Such items were used in crypts to ward off evil. The creature had to return home each night. It could only live in a place abandoned by men.

'Holy crap,' I said aloud, making several archive users look up and frown at me. *Abandoned by men*. Well, Viper's Green had pretty much been abandoned by everyone.

There was another relic listed in the haul removed from Libya. A spear. What else could it be but the spear that Perseus had used to kill the Gorgon? It was a special one, and you had to pierce the correct side of the creature to kill it. There was nothing about Perseus's shield. Maybe that had gone missing, or maybe it had just been any old shield – all it had to do was reflect the Gorgon's image. Attached to the next page was an extra note, again in old fountain pen handwriting that was really hard to read:

'*The crypt of St Patrick's at Viper's Green can no longer be opened. On the occasion of its last unsealing, a great calamity resulted in a number of deaths. Public outcry resulted in the crypt being permanently closed.*'

I checked the dates. One batch of strange deaths in the area had gone unnoticed because they had coincided with the Great Flu Epidemic of 1918–19. Loads of people died, so no one would have noticed the Gorgon's victims.

Max's father had opened the crypt. And his son had opened the gates to the park.

I knew I had to find Max and get there as soon as possible, before anyone else could be hurt.

On the way I passed the police station, and thought about going in. I stood there watching through the window, as the desk sergeant wrote some details onto his computer screen while this woman was crying her eyes out – and he was taking no notice at all, just typing, and I thought *That's what he'll do if I go in there. He'll just type and type, and ignore what's really happening.*

So I carried on past, to Max's flat.

18: Crazies

The Torrington Estate had probably looked grim and depressing in bright sunshine, back in the days when every flat had been occupied by a family. But emptied out, half-flooded and seen through driving grey rain, it looked like the most miserable place on earth.

I made my way across the sodden, dead soil of the quadrangle, and up towards Max's flat. I felt bad about the way we had parted. I reached the front door, but when I knocked there was no answer. Finally a woman's voice called out.

'All right, I'm coming! You don't have to knock the sodding door down.'

There in the doorway stood Max's mother. Jackie was still wearing her dressing gown and carpet slippers. She smelled of stale cigarettes and alcohol. Her mouth was heavy with bright red lipstick, but still seemed too thin until I realised that she hadn't put her false teeth in.

'He ain't here, all right? He's gone off somewhere.'

'Do you know where?' I asked, trying to avoid her sour breath.

'He don't tell me anything. He's supposed to leave me a note when he goes out. Those are the rules around here.'

'Are you sure he hasn't?'

'Don't know, do I? I can't look because I've lost me glasses and can't see nothing. If you see him, tell the little bugger he's in trouble again. He's going to grow up just like his father.' She shut the door with a bang.

'You'll never find him, you know, not unless he wants to be found.'

I turned around sharply to find Emma leaning against the stairwell, her face half-hidden in shadow. 'When he decides to disappear, no one can ever find him. He knows a million places to hide.'

'Are you OK?' I asked. Emma was holding her pale arm close to her side, as if in pain. She looked cold and tired.

'I haven't been sleeping well. It's this place. My mother...the moonlight bothers her. The last few nights, she's not been herself. She sees the moon from her window and gets crazy. Sometimes she starts crying. I go to bed and put my earplugs in. It's the only way I can get any sleep. She goes off, walking around, I don't know. These are strange times for us.'

She stepped into the light. I was shocked at how ill

and pale she looked. I wanted to put my arms around her and assure her that everything would be all right. When she looked at me, I felt different. Made special somehow. It was hard to explain. I wanted to make her smile again, as she had the night before. Now she seemed like a completely different person. Dealing with her mother all night was obviously upsetting her.

'I'm sorry she's causing so much trouble for you,' I said.

'Why would you care?' Emma replied sharply. 'Who am I to you? I don't know you, any more than you know me.'

'I was just trying to be friendly, that's all.'

'Yeh right, that's what boys always say. That's what they say to me, until they come back and see where I live. They see my minuscule bedroom and the crummy flat, and then they meet my mother who tells them she hears noises in the walls and thinks there's some crazy person inside her trying to get out. So pretty quickly they think it's all too much hard work, and they make excuses, any old excuse to get away.'

'You're right, Emma, I don't know you. But honest, I wouldn't do that to you.'

She appeared not to have heard me. 'I know about boys.' She spat the last word out at me. 'They divide girls up into groups. The ones they fancy, the ones who look easy, and the ones they're scared of. They chat you up then make you look bad to their mates.' She hugged herself and looked out at the falling rain. 'So go on, Mr Red Hellion, and tell all your mates you hang out with the daughter of the mad woman.'

'I'm not like them. I've got more respect for you. And so does Max. He cares a lot about you. He told me how much you and your mother helped his family, how you've been really good to him.'

'Did he also tell you about his father? About why Gary was always hanging around our flat? Gary told my mum he loved her. Ask her if you like, it's another one of her pet subjects. He said he'd leave his wife for her and she believed him. That's why she had a breakdown when he disappeared. Max knows, and he still covers up for his dad. So now two families are broken. And it goes on with men of every age, telling lies and laughing behind your back.'

I could see the pain in her dark eyes. 'You must try to get some sleep.'

Her face crumpled. She was close to tears. 'The nights – you got no idea how bad they are for us. We have to get out of here. I really dread the nights.'

'I'm sorry.'

'Yeah, well I don't need pity, right.'

Her honesty and bravery upset me. What kind of pressure was there on a girl who had to look after an increasingly crazy mother?

I knew I shouldn't leave her, but right now I had to find Max as soon as possible.

I went back down the steps of the stairwell, splashing away from the derelict corridors and balconies, leaving Emma behind in the shadows.

19: Slow Death

I knew where to find Max, and this time I made sure I would be ready for whatever happened. Ducking into the house and avoiding the usual questions thrown by my mum – 'Where have you been?', 'Have you eaten anything?' and 'Where do you think you're going?' – I packed a torch, a roll of nylon cord, matches and a can of lighter fluid. OK, there wasn't any logic to this choice, but I was in a hurry, and anything that would have been more useful was locked in the shed. If I'd been playing Death Hammer I'd have gathered better weapons: spear, laser blaster, nunchuks, energy capsules.

The rain had misted away the shops in the High Street. It looked as if part of a charcoal drawing had been smudged and erased. As I passed Nalin's corner store, I saw that the steel shutters were still down, something that had never happened in all the years Nalin and his father had run the place. It felt like the neighbourhood was slowly being robbed of people. An image entered my head: Viper's Green gradually filling with statues as the surrounding streets were emptied out.

The thought of going back inside the park for my third and hopefully final visit filled me with dread. I was pretty sure Max would be there looking for his father. Where else could he have gone? It was the only course of action left open to him. The Gorgon must return home each night, that was what the book said. Max had gone back to the crypt to wait for her. He didn't want me there now; I'd served my purpose.

As I stood outside the gate, I began to realize that Max had planned this from the start. He had needed someone to help him read his father's notes, the signs in the church, even the gravestones. How long had he stood there outside the gates, pretending to be breaking open the lock, waiting for some mug like me to come along?

I knew I should be angry at being tricked, but I felt sorry for him. Max was living in the fallout of his father's disappearance. He was lost, and had no one to turn to. If I deserted him as well, there would only be Emma left, and she had enough problems of her own. Pushing open the gates, I entered the park once more. As I passed beneath the dark canopy of the woods I felt my heart beat faster. Somewhere in here waited death, disease, destruction.

I reached the church more quickly this time. The route was becoming familiar to me. On the left was the fenced-off woodland, with its miserable little crypt filled with litter and rainwater. Ahead was the dead oak blocking the path. Beyond lay the broken church, its roof sagging and smashed, its gravestones defaced and cracked.

I listened carefully. Not for any unusual noise, but for the silence that would herald the arrival of the Gorgon. I felt sure that the creature was bothered by noise and daylight – that was why it stayed here in the gloom.

I heard raised voices coming from the back of the church. I knew at once that Max and Josun were having an argument. I ran down the side of the church, reaching the small brick extension where Josun lived. The caretaker was outside, striding about in front of Max as if he was getting ready to hit him.

'It had nothing to do with me,' he shouted. 'Your old man came here with some rubbish he'd heard about the park. Something some crazy woman told him about things from Libya being brought back here. You want the truth, sonny? He thought if he could find 'em, he'd make some money selling 'em. A nice way to earn a living, selling stuff stolen from a graveyard! How's that make you feel about your father, eh?'

'Take that back!' Max suddenly jumped at him. He had Josun by the throat, and the pair of them fell over into the long grass. Josun was making noises like a dog being strangled by its lead.

126

'Get off him!' I shouted, trying to pull them apart.

'You stay out of this, it's got nothing to do with you.'

Max fell to the ground as Josun pushed him off. The fight had exposed the caretaker's withered arm. Embarrassed, Josun pulled the sleeve of his boiler suit down over the brown stick-like bones.

The caretaker pulled himself upright and smoothed his straggling hair back in place. 'There was nothing left here,' he said, determined to set the record straight. 'There might have been once, a hundred years ago, but vandals smashed open the crypt and broke up everything inside it, and they kept on coming back and doing it until there was nothing left. Your dad thought there might still be something lying around. He wasn't the first bloke to think that. But there's nothing. I caught him digging under the slabs of the crypt, trying to find things he could sell to get him out of debt. I've seen that kind of light in people's eyes before, when they think there's money to be made out of nothing, and it's bloody pathetic.'

Max was silent now, but breathing hard. For a moment he looked as if he might cry. Then he pulled himself together.

'Come on,' I said, trying to take his arm. 'You don't need this. Let's get out of here.'

Max shoved me away. 'Leave me alone.'

'I'm not your enemy, Max. I know what you wanted, and I'm sorry you didn't find it. Leave this guy alone now. Let's go home. I have to tell you something.'

Max looked as if he might fight on, but as the rain got stronger the anger left him. He looked defeated. Rising and wiping the mud from his jeans, he turned away and walked off.

'I'm sorry,' I apologised to Josun. 'He shouldn't have attacked you, but he doesn't know what to do about his father.'

Josun had calmed down a little. He continued to rearrange his sleeve over his damaged arm.

'Why was his father digging around in the crypt? He didn't really expect to find something valuable, did he?'

'I don't know,' Josun admitted. 'There've always been stories about this place. It's because of the explorer bloke.'

'What explorer?'

'Sir Richard Torrington,' Josun explained. 'His name's everywhere. He owned this land and most of the houses nearby.'

I thought, *That's what it said in the archive. And it's why my street is called Torrington Avenue.*

'He was an archaeologist. Made a lot of discoveries in the Middle East. By the time he came back home he was sick and close to dying, so he was buried here at St Patrick's. Most of the stuff he'd dug up was given to the British Museum. But a few things were buried in the crypt with him.'

'Is he still here?'

'No. A few years ago his bones were moved to the family estate, along with the items he was buried with. Well, all except one, which he'd insisted should stay here. Crypts were supposed to be protected by something that wards off evil.'

'What was left behind?'

'It was nothing, just a cracked stone jar with an ugly face on the side. It had no value, and the people who came to take away the body didn't want it. I'm sorry for that boy and his father, but there's nothing else here.'

I thought maybe the jar was buried in the flooded floor of the crypt. Things were starting to make sense. If the Gorgon head on the side of the jar hadn't been recognized, nobody would ever have known it was a valuable relic, the actual *Gorgoneion*. People went missing from Viper's Green, and some while later the council closed down the park. I was willing to bet that the first disappearance happened pretty soon after the crypt was opened.

I knew I had to ask. 'Do you ever feel there's something here with you in the park? Something not quite human?'

'I don't want to talk about that. It's nothing to do with me.' The caretaker began to head back to his house.

'But you know it's there.'

'Of course I do.' Embarrassed, he moved his withered arm away so that I couldn't look at it.

'You saw it, didn't you? You didn't look in its eyes,

but you caught a small glimpse of it, enough to damage your arm. You know about the Gorgon.'

'I don't know what it's called. It wasn't anything you'd want to see. But I know it's bad. I saw it explode a bunch of squirrels once.' In any other circumstances I would have laughed, but it didn't seem quite so funny here in the gloom.

'Those people in the wood, they're not statues.'

'I don't go near them, and nor should you.'

'They're people who died because the Gorgon looked at them. It peered deep into their eyes and they were turned to stone – it's some kind of chemical process I don't understand.'

'No, they don't die, not straight away,' said Josun bitterly, glancing down at his dried-up fingers. 'Their skin changes its structure. It hardens and imprisons them. They suffer a living death. They dry up inside their own bodies. I don't know how long it takes. Sometimes seconds, sometimes hours, sometimes days. Their innards are still soft at first. Their vocal cords still work. I've heard them out there in the dark, crying, begging to be killed, but there's nothing I can do for them.'

'You could have told someone. You might have been able to save them.'

'If I'd have brought the police and their scientists in here, do you think it would have let me live? It would have come after me. It isn't human. It's got no feelings, no emotions. It's like a snake in every way. Cold, cruel,

130

dead. And when you disturb a snake, when you corner it, that's when it strikes out. So get out now, go away from here!' The old man began to shout, waving me away. 'It can hear every word that's spoken in this place. You'll make it angry. I don't want any more trouble.'

I was sure the creature had left Josun alone because he had loyally guarded the crypt and the church for so long. But it had looked upon his arm and withered it, as a warning.

I ran after Max. 'Wait!' I called, catching up with him by the fallen oak. 'Wait, I have to talk to you. It's going to sound totally, *totally* stupid but you need to listen. The explorer, Sir Richard Torrington, he was buried with the *Gorgoneion*, a stone jar with the head of the Gorgon carved on its side. It was used in crypts to ward off evil spirits. I think the monster was connected with the jar. It was the last place anyone would expect to look, and then it got released somehow. I don't know how. We know the Gorgon was killed thousands of years earlier – but what if it can regenerate, you know, grow itself back, just like a snake does when it loses its tail? It came back and the people started disappearing.'

'Yeh, whatever.' Max carried on walking. 'Nobody cares about ancient history. It's all a load of made--up bollocks.'

'It's not, don't you see? This is about your father. Emma gave me the clue when she said that Gary had been in love with her mother. He was supposed to take her away and then he never showed up.'

'Great, so my old man was a liar as well as a thief. If you got any other good news for me, keep it to yourself.'

'He wasn't either of those things, Max. What if he found the jar – the *Gorgoneion* – in the crypt and removed it? And the Gorgon came back to life and attacked him? That's why he never went back for Emma's mum.'

'Then where's his body, smart-arse? The other stone bodies are all here, aren't they? Why isn't he?'

'I don't know. I just know he wasn't a bad man. Come on, let's get out of this rain. I'm fed up with being wet all the time. I got new trainers and they're full of water now.'

We trudged through the park in silence, but I was worried. It felt as if I was missing a piece of the puzzle. If Max's father wasn't in the park, where did he go? What had happened to him?

There were too many questions I had no way of answering, and all the time I felt the creature was moving closer. It was as though the spectre of the Gorgon was haunting us all.

20: Encrusted

We'd almost reached the gates when Max stopped in his tracks and patted his neck. 'Damn.'

'What's the matter?'

'Gary's chain. The shark tooth. It was still around my neck a few minutes ago. It must have come off when I started fighting with Josun.'

'You want to go back for it?'

'It's the only thing I have from my old man.'

'You picked a lousy time to lose something. Come on then. But let's be quick.' We clambered back over the dead oak, and followed the path to the church once more – into the spot where no daylight could ever reach. But as we drew close, the hairs started to prickle on the back of my neck. *Not now*, I thought.

The sound in the surrounding trees was dying away to a numbing silence.

'It's here,' I whispered. 'Can't you feel it?'

I was right. The sound of birds, traffic and even falling rain had faded. Max pushed aside a branch and looked through to the shadowed church grounds.

'Can you see anything?'

'No. It looks OK.'

We went into the graveyard, walking as quietly as possible. The deadening effect was all around us now.

Max moved slowly and carefully, shifting around to one side of the great stone church. We saw it at the same time; the back view of a tall figure in greenish rags, hunched over something that lay on the ground between the graves. It was just like the creature I had seen attacking Gabriel and Nalin in my dream-visions.

'Is that it?' Max whispered.

'It's the Gorgon.'

As we crept forward, we saw that the creature was standing on the exact spot where Max had fought with Josun. I grabbed Max's arm, but Max shook me free and moved closer, as if the sight of the Gorgon had cast a spell upon him.

'Max, come back,' I called as loudly as I dared, but he kept going.

The creature sensed someone was behind it. Unfolding itself and rising to its full height, it revealed the back of its head. Even at this distance, I could see the mass of writhing snakes, so green and shiny that they looked wet. Cocking its head to one side and listening, it started to turn. The snakes rolled as it tilted its head.

I threw myself at Max, knocking him off his feet. I stuck my hand across his mouth and held him down in the long grass between the graves. My instinct was to look up and see what was happening. But I knew that the Gorgon would strike me to stone if I did so.

Max struggled to get free, but I held him tightly in place. 'You mustn't look into its eyes,' I hissed. 'If you do, you're dead.'

We waited, hardly daring to breathe. *How can we protect ourselves if we can't look to see where it is?* I asked myself. *We need to know where it's going.*

I heard footsteps splashing through water. There was a gap between each splash, as if it was striding and stopping; the creature seemed in no hurry, merely curious about who was on its land.

I knew I had to look ahead, but I limited the view by peering through the gap in my fingers. Slowly I raised myself and checked the tops of the bushes in my sight. But while I was doing this, Max suddenly jumped up and broke cover. He ran for the ground where the creature had been standing.

'Red!' he called. 'Come on!'

Without daring to look, I blundered forward over the limestone graves, keeping my eyes trained on the ground.

I found myself standing beside Josun's body. The caretaker was turning to stone, but he was still alive. I watched in horror as the dark crystals scabbed over his blistered skin. I fell to my knees and tried to tear away an oval piece of stone that had formed on the side of Josun's face, but as it came off it took the skin with it. Underneath was a blood-filled mess of burned tissue. As soon as this was exposed to the air, it became stony.

Josun was making terrible rasping noises, as if his throat was filling with gravel. He tried to bring his good hand up to his neck, but pieces of skin were cracking and falling away, leaving raw patches. The caretaker had landed on his withered arm, which had cracked and broken apart to expose bones and tendons.

Now, as the pair of us watched in horror, Josun's tongue turned brown and splintered. The stone virus was spreading into his throat. His eyes turned yellow with pus and sank back into their sockets. Something red and sticky was leaking from his left ear. Then the whole ear dropped off, exposing the white bone of his skull underneath.

He coughed, and his throat split open. There was a series of cracks as the skin of his stomach popped apart, like a shirt that was too tight and losing its buttons. His innards were soaking through his boiler suit. We could see his beating heart. The exposed veins and valves scabbed over with grey moss.

'Keep away from him!' I warned. 'It could spread to you.'

Josun's outstretched arm tried to grab at us, but then it froze in mid air and fell back. Moments later, he was dead.

We heard the Gorgon moving behind us. I rose to my feet and glanced down into the puddles of water. 'Look,' I told Max, 'we can see it.'

The tall green figure was six metres away from us, facing in our direction, waiting for us to look up into its eyes. It was human nature to want to look. Wasn't that always the first thing you did when you met someone, the only way you could ever trust them?

You always look into their eyes.

The Gorgon was in no rush to catch its prey. It stood there silent and very still, and waited for us to look.

It was like having an itch you needed to scratch, and the longer you tried not to do it, the worse it got. It was so quiet and still. I suddenly got the idea that it was trying to hypnotize us.

I looked over at Max, and I saw him starting to look up.

21: Enemy Visible

Luckily a smack on the head cured him of that, although he nearly clouted me back. 'What do we do?' Max whispered. 'It's right on the path. It's doing what snakes do, like in *The Jungle Book*. I feel like I need to look. I can't stop myself.'

'You have to.' I put my hands over Max's eyes, but I could feel it too. 'Come on. If you look, the same thing will happen to you that happened to Josun. We'll have to go around the long way.'

'We'll get lost and it'll come after us.'

'Not if we keep to the wall of the park we won't. We can't stay here.'

The Gorgon remained as motionless as one of its statue-victims. I knew that if it was really like a snake it would strike suddenly, when we were least expecting it to.

'Come on.' I grabbed Max's arm and pulled him away. We moved behind Josun's body. Max saw his father's neck-chain lying on the grass and slipped from my hold. He ran back for the chain.

'Leave it!' I called out in desperation.

'I can't do that,' he answered.

And Max looked up. He was caught between the chain and the Gorgon.

The great snake-creature made its move. Its ragged robes blurred about it, and the air was filled with the sound of boiling, hissing snakes. It didn't act like before, freezing Max with a poisonous stare. Instead it fell upon him like an actual snake, snapping and biting at his exposed neck. The wriggling serpents on its head turned and struck together, all at once, a hundred of them straining to find a space on his flesh where they could sink their fangs.

They pulled, stretched, bit and clung on.

Max tried to cry out, but the Gorgon smothered him, dropping over his body and covering it to prevent its victim's escape. Some of the longer serpents on the back of its neck knotted themselves around Max's throat, pinning him in place while the snakes drew back and struck, again and again.

Powerless to help, I glimpsed the strike from the puddles at my feet. I didn't dare to look at the creature's back in case it suddenly turned around and froze me with its deadly stare. There was nothing I could do to save Max. When the Gorgon finally rose, it turned around and came at me.

I did the only thing I could think of. I stepped back – into a shaft of sunlight that fell between the tree branches.

The Gorgon was a creature of the dark. It could not advance any closer. I looked down into the puddles and saw its angry stare. Finally, it slid away through the cover of the trees. The hissing faded and normal sound returned.

I turned my attention back to Max. I knew he was already sinking into the grip of death.

There would be no miraculous last-minute recovery for him. His face was swollen and black with venom. His eyes were shut tight in pain. His thickened tongue thrust from his foaming mouth. His hands tightly clutched tufts of grass and earth. Yet as I watched, Max's features softened and he looked weirdly calm. Eternal sleep, wasn't that what death was often called? I could see it now; my friend was passing into another place. He was completely still.

Feeling sick, I removed my jacket and gently laid it over his face. Then I picked up Max's bag. I dropped the shark tooth chain inside it.

There was nothing else I could do for the time being. I had failed us both. I ran from the park, vaulting over the dead oak, and never dared to look behind, to where my brief friendship with Max had begun and ended.

22: A Place Forsaken

It wasn't supposed to have happened.

The pair of us should have tackled the Gorgon and beaten it. Wasn't that what always happened in movies? Instead, poor Max had died a gruesome death, trying to retrieve the only thing his father had ever given him.

I didn't want to leave him there, but I couldn't drag him out by myself. All I could think to do right now was go and fetch his mother. I headed to the Torrington Estate with Max's bag heavy in my hands. Into the deserted grounds. Across the flooded quadrangle. Splashing down the ground floor tunnels leading to the dark stairwells.

A huddled brown ball of rags jumped out of the shadows with a cry of fright. A sleeping tramp and I had managed to scare the life out of each other. I reached the first floor staircase and ran to the landing above, then checked myself.

Calm down, what are you doing? Where are you going? You can't tell Max's mother what happened, she'll go nuclear on you. Besides, the police will want to know what happened, how you're involved. They'll know anyway, because you stupidly left your jacket at the scene. They'll be able to identify you. What are you going to do?

Think.

Think.

You're not Perseus. You're not a hero. You're just a teenager. But you must find a way to end this now. You have to do it for Max. You have to make his death the end of it all.

I closed my eyes and leaned my head on the rain-streaked concrete pillar beside me. I tried not to recall Max's final moments, his snake-bitten face bloating and blackening with poison. Remembering Max's bag, I unzipped it and turned it out onto the wet landing floor.

Not exactly a treasure-house of possessions. The shark tooth, which looked ridiculously fake and plastic in daylight. A filthy blue baseball cap with a Navy Seals logo. An iPod Shuffle that looked as if it had been trodden on by an elephant. An old photo of Max, his father and mother in happier times, standing awkwardly in a row. His mother was squinting into the sun, shielding her eyes. Behind them, some kids were playing with a Frisbee.

I suddenly realized that the picture had been taken here on the Torrington Estate, before everyone had started to leave. Looking at the dark threatening buildings now, it was hard to imagine that laughter and sunlight had ever reached down to the residents.

The other thing I found was the packet of notes from Max's father.

I unfolded the map to the crypt and laid it out on the concrete. Poor old Gary really couldn't draw. Max had a single stick of gum in the bottom of his backpack. I hated gum, but now I opened it and chewed it. I looked out into the falling rain. It dripped from the weed-sown terraces, poured from broken gutters and leaked through the ceilings of the underpasses.

I thought of the few people left here; Max's mother, drinking herself to death, crying over her missing husband. I thought of Emma, angry and cheated and hurt, hating the boys from the estate. Diane, her mother, waiting for Gary to rescue her, and becoming too mad to leave her room, except at night. I wanted to see my own parents, even my sister, just to remind myself what a normal family was like. I wanted to speak to my dad, just to hear his voice.

The brick pillars that supported the three terraced floors of the block were cracked and falling apart. I could see the problem. They were too widely spaced to support the balconies. They had been cheaply built and badly repaired, because it didn't matter if these families lived in lousy conditions. People like them weren't important. The thought made me angry.

I looked back at the map of the crypt site, then up at the estate. Slowly, I stopped chewing.

The truth dawned on me.

Why didn't I see it before?

I needed to get up onto the highest point of the estate.

The lifts were broken, so I climbed the stairs to the top floor and peered over the edge of the balcony at the quadrangle.

I compared what I saw to Gary's map. The two shapes were exactly the same.

Gary, I thought, *you weren't such a bad artist after all. You weren't drawing the churchyard at Viper's Green. You were drawing a map of the estate where you and your family lived!*

Max's father had sketched a nest of snakes and marked the centre with the letter C. But what if it wasn't a 'C' for Crypt? What if it was a 'G' for *Gorgoneion*, the engraved stone jar that was kept in the crypt to protect its contents? And what if Gary had found it in the crypt and brought it back to the estate? Where would he have hidden it? Had the Gorgon followed him back? That made no sense, because the jar was meant to ward the creature off, not attract it. What had really happened on the day he'd opened the crypt?

Turning the paper around, I followed the line of the walls it marked. I now knew where to go.

Keeping the page in front of me, I ran back down the stairs, through the dark network of underpasses. The

144

estate had become a far more disturbing place than the church. I passed through deepening shadows, heading into the dingy corner where two great crumbling apartment blocks met.

Max's father had drawn a small square, with a further enclosed space behind it. I stood at the junction and looked about. I saw a concrete corridor stretching off in each direction. Black pools of rain shone like oil slicks beneath the sputtering neon lights.

From somewhere far above me, I could hear the sound of water steadily pouring onto metal sheeting. I looked back into the corner, and noticed that a tall steel door stood partially open. Taking my torch from my bag, I clicked it on and entered the room beyond the door.

It was really warm inside. I was in the boiler room for the building. Six tall tanks in red plastic sleeves stood in a row, but only one of them was hot. The council probably hated having to heat any of them, but while there were still families living on the estate they had no choice.

The second room – the last one marked on Gary's drawing – was filled with huge steel pipes. The conduits carried the hot water to the apartments above. There was a strangely familiar zoo smell in here, earthy and sharp. I shone the torch across the bare floor, and made a mental list of everything I saw. Some rusty metal sheets. Bits of plywood stacked against the wall. A lethal-looking garden rake. A bicycle with a twisted wheel. Several folding chairs. A broken-backed sofa thick with mildew. Piles of stinking grey-green rags, swirled in a great oily heap.

I ventured further in, sensing that I had arrived at my destination. I was inside the lair of the Gorgon. This was why Gary had made the map; he had wanted his son to know where to look if anything bad happened to him.

There was something on top of the pile of rags. A fragment of orange-coloured stone with a corner of a wild face carved on it. My torch beam lit up a face, a spiny tooth, a single strand of snake-hair.

The *Gorgoneion*. Just a small piece of the jar. I moved closer to take a look.

Outside, I could hear the rain pounding down harder than ever. A storm was breaking above the abandoned estate. I moved the torch beam back and forth. There was something coiled underneath the sofa. At first I thought it was an old inner tube.

Slowly and carefully, I pushed back the edge of the sofa and shone the torch beneath it.

Something glittered darkly back.

The viper pattern was clear, the pale inverted V shapes standing out against shiny sepia scales.

The biggest, longest, fattest snake I had ever seen in my life.

23: The Graeae

I realized I was looking at a huge snakeskin that had been shed.

Snakes cast off their skins and grow new ones. Everything was starting to make sense. The *Gorgoneion* had held the remains of the original Gorgon. That was why the superstitions said it could ward off other harmful spirits; they were afraid of it. Gary had found the pot in the bottom of the crypt. It was flooded down there now, so it looked empty, but he hadn't been afraid to search beneath the filthy water – that was why no one else had found anything lately. He had brought it back here. More importantly, he had opened it and found the only surviving remains of the Gorgon itself.

Perseus had killed the creature, and had put its skin in the jar. Suddenly it didn't seem like a Greek myth at all, just a man killing an animal and saving its hide as a trophy.

I guessed Gary hadn't wanted to put it in his flat because of the risk it might pose to his family.

I wanted to touch the skin but something stopped me. Suppose just a scratch from the Gorgon's scales was enough to reactivate the kind of virus that could bring the monster back to life? I imagined germs in the skin that could spread a living Gorgon strain. Germs that reproduced in a healthy body, to take someone over and change them...

And worse still – it had happened before. Gary hadn't been the first to find the snakeskin. Others had touched it and had become infected. They had disappeared.

I thought it through. What if the being that was stalking the streets at night carried the strain in its blood? Then each full moon the creature shed its human skin somehow to become the Gorgon once more, just like Medusa changed. It stalked its victims, killing them, crushing them, turning them to stone. It sucked the life from its prey and stored their dried husks in Viper's Green, from where it had been released. And at night it slept here in its new warm home – snakes liked the warmth. They were cold-blooded, and needed to absorb heat.

If this was happening, then no one else knew the truth but me. And no one else could stop it. Oh, *man*, I didn't want to be a modern-day Perseus. I never even got picked for football. Craig Sharwood got picked before me, and he had one leg shorter than the other. I couldn't be a hero.

Wait. Somebody else knew what was going on, because they carried the ancient virus. But who was it? I thought of Max's mother, clouding her mind with drink in the darkened bedroom of her flat. What was she so afraid of?

And then there was Emma's mother, locked in her room, creeping out at night, as mad as a hatter. What had made her lose her senses?

The two women were friends. Had they confided in one another? Hadn't there been a third who had died? Three women, made old before their time. There was something Max had told me – I couldn't quite reach it in my mind, something in the past that held the key…

I ran from the boiler room and out into the corridor. The cold air that hit me was like someone throwing open a freezer door. I carried on across the quadrangle and up the staircase on the other side, to where Emma and her mother lived. I hammered on the door, but it took ages for anyone to answer.

'All right, I'm coming.' Emma looked as if she had been asleep. Her hair was matted and messed up. She sounded more tired than ever. 'I thought it would be you. Did you find him?'

I didn't deliberately choose to lie to her; it just seemed the best thing to do for the moment. 'No, I can't find him anywhere.'

'Yeh, well, he sometimes takes off without telling anyone.'

'Is your mother in?' *Stupid*, I thought, *stupid because she never goes out by day.*

'Yeh, she's in her room but she's trying to sleep. She's taken some pills, more than she usually takes.'

'I need to speak to her. It's really important.'

'She won't want to talk to you, Max. She doesn't like strangers. They frighten her. She's blind.'

'What, you mean—'

'Yeh, as in she can't see?'

Of course, I thought, *it all makes sense now. History repeats itself, myths keep happening over and over, that's why they become myths.*

'Her friend, the one who died – was she blind as well?'

'Who, old Iris? She was partially sighted. Funny, having a name like Iris and being blind in one eye. She had an accident when she was a kid, fell off her bike and hit a fence. A splinter of wood went right through her left pupil. And Max's mum is so short-sighted she can hardly see a thing. You should have seen the three of them, Diane, Iris and Jackie, walking along like three blind mice.'

When I had last seen Jackie she had complained of not being able to see without her glasses, and she had not put her false teeth in. I wondered if Iris was also missing her teeth. The *Graeae*, the three women who knew how to defeat the Gorgon, only had one eye and one tooth between them. Was it just coincidence that Jackie, Iris and Diane seemed like their modern-day versions?

'Let me talk to her, Emma. Please.'

'All right, but only if you leave as soon as you've seen her.' She led the way along the thinly carpeted hall. 'It's the first door on the left. If she screams the place down when she hears you, that's not my problem, OK?'

I reached the door and waited outside, listening. No sound came from within. I knocked and waited. Finally, I tried the handle.

Emma's mother was sitting facing the window, as if looking out onto the square. But the curtains were closed, and she was staring at nothing.

'I thought you might come up,' she said slowly turning around. My mouth fell open in surprise. She was beautiful. Her unlined face was kind and as sad as her daughter's.

'I could hear you talking downstairs. When I open my eyes all I can see is the vaguest of shapes. The doctor says it's in my mind, not physical at all. Did you know that could happen?'

'Is it all right if I talk to you for a minute?'

'You'll have to be quick. I need to sleep. I'm so tired.' She muttered something under her breath.

'Sorry?'

She cleared her throat. 'This is all my fault.'

'I don't understand. What is?'

151

'Oh, *everything*. To begin with, I should never have fallen in love.' She changed the subject. 'I'm sorry the room is a mess. I'm supposed to set an example to my daughter, and instead she has to look after me. Tell me, do you like her?'

'She's OK.'

'She's a good girl, and she needs good friends. I can't take care of myself any more, let alone her.'

She was obviously upset and I felt I was in the way, but she suddenly pointed in my direction, jabbing her finger, like she could see me. 'I think you know who I am.' She leaned forward, her voice as dry and whispery as tissue paper. 'I've been made sightless because I'm one of the grey. Is that the right word?'

'*Graeae*,' I corrected. 'How long have you known?'

She appeared not to have heard me. 'We were great friends, the three of us.'

'Iris and Jackie, you mean?'

'Of course. There was poor old Iris, silly Jackie, and me. All a bit in love with the same man, but me most of all.'

'Gary.'

'Max's father was a real charmer, all right. But he's gone now.' She pulled her threadbare cardigan more tightly over her shoulders. 'Everything went wrong. Now there's nothing I can do to put it right. Pass me my drink.'

I handed her the tumbler from her dresser, and waited while she drained it. 'What happened?' I asked.

'Gary said he was going to leave his wife, and run away with Emma and me. He was going to bring Max, too. We were going to live abroad. A new happy family. Spain, perhaps, or better still, Greece – more appropriate, don't you think? You'll need money to do that, I told him. He said he'd found something in the church that would make us rich. He went to get it—'

'And never came back.'

'No, he came back, and hid it here. Then the horrors started.'

'But he died.'

'Yes, he died, because of what he'd brought home with him.'

'The *Gorgoneion*.'

'The thing in the jar. He should never have taken it.'

'The jar contained a snakeskin, didn't it? But how—'

'Give me your hand.'

I'd never been so close to a blind person before, but she made me feel calm. She took my hand and smiled. 'I think perhaps you're sensitive to the strangeness in the world. That's why you came. Some people can sense more than others.'

'I don't know what you mean.' I removed my hand. 'Do you think it's real?'

'It's an ancient force that somehow came back to life, yes. It can kill, or make people sick.'

'Did Gary bring anything else back from the churchyard apart from the jar with the snakeskin? Did he leave anything here for you to look after?'

'No. There's no spear, and no shield, if that's what you're thinking. This isn't some story you just learn at school, these are our lives, and nothing goes the way it's supposed to. There are no real heroes. The stories are based in fact, but you can't believe everything that's in them.'

'But there must be something—'

'Nothing can stop it now. It's getting more powerful each night. I don't have the strength to keep it away. When the time comes, we can only do what we are fated to do.'

I didn't understand what she meant. I went downstairs, but there was no sign of Emma. As I left I looked back at her mother, staring from the curtained window with sightless blue eyes, and tears streaming down her pale, smooth cheeks.

By the time I got home, the strangeness of my meeting with Emma's mum had worn off and I felt kind of stupid. Walking into my own house made things feel more normal again.

A spear and a shield were the only weapons that could kill the Gorgon. I tried to think what I could use. Where could you find shields and spears any more? A museum? What was I supposed to do, head for the local hardware store and ask if they stocked different sized shields?

The light was starting to fade. The Gorgon would soon be out looking for its next victim. It had to keep attacking – that's what it was designed to do, like any other wild animal. A reptile had no emotions, only an unstoppable instinct. All I could do now was try not to panic and wait for its arrival. I had no plan other than to follow it, corner it and try to – I don't know, stab it or something. I would kill it for Max. I could only hope that when the time came, I would somehow stay calm and think of the right weapon to use.

I didn't dare to fall asleep again, because of what I might see. Instead, I settled down to wait.

24: Undefeatable

And so we're back to where we came in. With me in my bedroom, and the creature waiting outside in the night.

Now I was heading downstairs, going to the front door, stepping out into the strange bubble of silence that followed the creature wherever it went. I couldn't see the Gorgon, but I knew it was there, somewhere ahead in the falling rain, passing beneath the yellow streetlamps, looking for a new victim.

It walked with a steady beat, slowly turning its head this way and that, watching and listening. Those flat yellow-green eyes sensed the heat of humans. It felt no emotion, no love, no hate, no anger, no fear, nothing. It had the needs of a reptile, the need for daytime warmth and night-time food, but there was something more inside it – the need to kill for the sake of it. To suck up power the way a mosquito sucked blood from humans.

I knew this now. I kept well behind, travelling in its wake. I was scared of what might happen if I messed up. If I didn't kill it, the streets would continue to empty of people, just like the flats on the Torrington Estate had darkened one by one. The shops would close but no one would notice what was really happening, because no one believed it could really happen.

I ran on over the wet pavements, trying to gain distance between myself and the creature. Turning into the High Street, I knew I was closer. I passed Nalin's corner grocery, still shuttered and locked – had no one discovered that he'd become a victim?

I passed the Hen Hut, the Laundromat, the betting shop Gabriel would never come out of again. These were places I had known for years, but now everything was unfriendly and strange.

The silence began to get thicker.

I was getting close. I turned the next corner and saw it.

The creature was passing Bluston's Gowns, an old-fashioned ladies' clothing shop. The store had a double front, two great windows lined with floor-to-ceiling mirrors, and battered old dummies that faced each other.

I saw the Gorgon's reflection, repeated to infinity between the spotlit mirrors. It seemed hypnotized by its own grotesque image.

The great green head shifting and crawling with thin angry serpents.

The sickly face partly covered in translucent scales. The long claw-arms held at its sides.

The Gorgon opened its mouth and the white spines of its teeth were thrust out like those of a deep sea angler fish. The split tongue flickered in and out. The anchored snakes that sprouted from its skull bit at each other in a frenzy.

I figured the stone virus had no effect on the creature when it viewed its own form in a mirror. There went my only big idea – to try and get it to stare into its own eyes.

The green head tilted this way and that, angering the snakes. The yellow-green eyes remained fixed on the mirrors. Did it hate what it saw? Did it even recognize what it had become? Was it disgusted, pleased, horrified by the transformation? There was no way of understanding that blank face, any more than there was of seeing a smile on a snake, and yet I somehow knew that it was in terrible pain.

While I'd been waiting for the Gorgon to reappear, I'd searched the internet for hours, studying everything I could to find out more about the legend. According to Greek mythology, any blood drawn from the right side of the Gorgon's body could bring the dead back to life, but blood taken from the left was a strong poison. Could it be used to bring Max back? And if so, how quickly did I have to act for it to work? Surely I had left it too late...

The more I had read, the more confused I got. No two versions of the story matched. I used to be good at history, but that was because it was in books. This was living stuff, and weirder to deal with.

The Gorgon was here in modern-day London. Gary had taken the jar home, and a dead snakeskin had somehow created a living, breathing, mythical creature.

I heard a sharp hiss, and my first instinct was to look up, but I knew it had seen me. I had nothing to fight with. For now, I could only get away as fast as I could. I ran.

Some warrior, I told myself, pounding back through the rainy streets, *some great hero you are. 'When the time comes, we can only do what we are fated to do.' Why did I listen to the ravings of a crazy woman? I'm not Perseus. There are no real heroes. There is no shield or spear. The Gorgon is some kind of nightmare. And the horror will continue, because it was never meant to come back into the modern world like this.*

And I'm not strong enough to stop it.

THURSDAY

25: Shedding Skin

On Thursday the weather was supposed to improve, but the rain continued to fall. It was an INSET day, so there was no school. I hid away in my bedroom, knowing there was nothing I could do to stop the Gorgon. I needed a plan. Lucy and my Mum were going to visit an elderly uncle in Croydon and wanted me to come with them, but I managed to get out of it. I didn't like going there anyway, because his house smelled weird.

I watched them leave from the window, knowing that they were at least safely out of the Gorgon's hunting ground.

If only I knew how the shield and the spear could stop the Gorgon, I thought, *maybe I could find a modern version of them. There must be something about it on the net.* But here I realized the limits of reading. There comes a point where you have to go out and do things for yourself. I couldn't settle anywhere, so I grabbed my backpack and left the house.

I went up to the steel footbridge over the railway to see if I could spot anything left of Nalin. I needed to prove that my visions were real. I couldn't see anything from the bridge, so I went back down and ducked through the broken end of the fence, keeping beyond the security camera that I knew was positioned above the track.

The bank was slippery with all the rain we'd had, but I wanted to get up close. I couldn't see anything lying around, but it was hard to tell; the track is covered with chunks of gravel, and I supposed any one of them could have been a bit of Nalin.

Then I saw it, one piece darker at the centre than the rest. Checking that there were no trains coming, I got close and dropped to my knees. I didn't want to touch it, so I poked it with a pen. When I turned the chunk over, I realised there was an eye on the other side. Nalin's left eye.

With a yelp, I shot back up the embankment and headed for the Torrington Estate. I knew that the Gorgon visited its hiding place in the boiler room, probably resting there at night. The thought came to me that I might kill it while it slept. But how, and with what?

Anyway, none of this was how it was supposed to happen. The hero should storm the den of the creature and slice off its head. Isn't that what happened in the movie versions? But Perseus had been armed with a sword, not a spear. And he had used the shield to deflect arrows she had fired at him. The problem with ancient myths was that they became exaggerated in the retelling, until you couldn't get at the truth any more.

I found myself walking through the open-sided corridor that bordered the estate's litter-covered square.

'I told you it would be a waste of time talking to my mother. She's completely bonkers.' I looked up and found Emma leaning in her usual position against the concrete pillar of the stairwell, like a lookout at a sentry-post. Her face was slanted in shadows.

'Is she all right?'

'Yeah. She tries to take sleeping pills all the time, but I switch them for anti-diarrhoea medication. You'd think she'd have noticed by now. She hasn't been to the toilet in weeks. I'm trying to save her from herself.'

'And the blindness – it's not permanent?'

'No. She's always been a bit of a drama queen. Other mums just get fed up, but mine has to go blind. The doctor wants her to have therapy. He thinks they'll be able to sort it out.'

'I didn't understand what she was talking about,' I admitted. 'I wanted to tell her something, but couldn't bring myself to do it. But I have to explain it to you. Max is dead.'

'Oh God – where is he?'

'In the park. I had to leave him there. There was nothing I could do.'

'I had a terrible feeling about him. What happened?'

'It's a long story, and I'm not sure how much of it you're going to believe. You'd better sit down while I explain.'

She didn't seem keen on hearing the truth, but looked away instead. 'Poor Max, always so angry and rushing into things. We'll have to tell someone.'

'He went back to get his neck-chain and was attacked.'

'He shouldn't have gone. It said *Made in China* on the back. Not worth saving.'

Her odd reaction had me confused. I realized she thought he'd been beaten up. 'You don't sound very sad.'

She shrugged. 'Of course I'm sad. I'm just not that surprised. He was kind of crazy. All I have to do is close my eyes to see him again. Don't need a memory-stick for that, not when there's one inside my head. He's really dead?'

'Yes.'

'Then I suppose I'll cry at some point but I'm not going to do it in front of you.'

'You should leave this place, Emma. It's messing all of you up.'

She looked out at the rain. 'I was born here. I like it better without all the other people. Just me and Max.'

'But he's gone, and so has Gary, who was going to take you and your mother away from here.'

'Maybe they brought it on themselves. Most people do, I think. Gary should never have removed the Gorgon's jar from the crypt.'

'You know about that?'

'Of course. He brought it home and showed us. He came and set it down on the kitchen table, covered in some old rags he'd found. Thought he was going to make some easy money out of his big find. He hadn't even looked at it, so I looked for him. Inside there was just a huge, manky old snakeskin. It was like a thousand years old, but it still felt sticky.'

'You touched it!'

'Yeah, I pulled the skin out of its jar and wrapped it around my arm because it was actually kind of cool. I was going to take a picture on my phone. Gary told me off. He said I was damaging something rare and valuable. It was just an old snakeskin.'

'But it wasn't.'

'The weird thing was I had trouble pulling it off my arm. See?' She stepped from the shadows and showed me her pale right arm. I could now see a crimson scar winding all the way to her elbow. 'I thought it would heal but it hasn't, so I usually put make-up on it. The edge of the skin cut me as I tried to pull it off. Gary and Diane thought I should go to the hospital for a tetanus shot, they said there could be germs on it, but I didn't go.'

'Did it make you sick?'

'Yeh, how did you know?' She stepped into the light. 'That night, I started to feel feverish. I poured sweat. The room was stifling. I threw up something green and slimy. My eyes were yellow, like the time I had jaundice. But the next day I was fine, although I felt very tired and slept a lot. Gary delayed our trip until I was better. I think he was looking for an excuse, anyway.

'But when it got dark, I grew hot again. My temperature jumped. Gary called the doctor, but he wouldn't come out to the estate because the last time he was here someone slashed his car tyres. My skin felt tight. I wanted to break it open and step out from inside. How weird is that? Do you think I picked up some kind of bug from it?'

'You!' I took a step backwards in horror and almost fell. It was all starting to make sense. Emma was the Gorgon, but she didn't even know it. That was how the virus worked. It crept up on people as slowly and as silently as a snake.

Emma was looking at me in puzzlement. She took a step towards me.

'Red, what are you talking about? What's the matter?'

'I want to help, Emma, but I don't know what to do without hurting you.'

'What do you mean? I don't understand. Where are you going?'

I was shaking and trying to stall for time. 'Emma, I have to go and figure this out.'

'Wait! Gary's gone. Max is dead. We have nothing left. What's the matter? What's wrong?' She sounded desperate.

Part of me wanted to hold her, to say that everything would somehow be all right, but the familiar icy feeling was prickling the back of my neck.

Now she was backing away from me into the stony shadows and the night, and when I looked up again she had vanished.

26: Spear and Shield

I ran through the rain to the gates of Viper's Green. Now I knew that Emma was the Gorgon, the only way I could ever free her was by killing her. But I needed weapons, and I had an idea.

Right from the first time I ever saw them, I had been puzzled by the gates of Viper's Green. The sharp iron central railing was shaped like a dagger at the top. My mum had once told me they were more than a hundred years old. Could the gate have been put in during the time of Sir Richard Torrington? Had he put the gate there for a reason, to ward off evil and keep intruders from discovering the *Gorgoneion*?

I studied the gate, a row of black gold-topped spears set in iron strips, and tried each one in turn. The central one that held the gate in place was the longest, and it was loose, as if it had been waiting for someone to move it all these years. After making sure that there was no one coming, I worked it free. I had hardly seen anyone around in days. It was as if they all sensed something terrible was happening, and were locking themselves indoors.

The tip of the spear was covered in layers of paint. It was so long, and so heavy that I had to drag it along the floor. Not caring what I would say if anyone stopped me, I hauled it home. Then I took it down to my dad's old shed, and broke the lock off the door. I used an electric grinder and an ordinary file on the point to make it sharp again. Once it was gleaming I tried it on my thumb, and watched as a thin trickle of blood ran over my hand.

The shield needed a bit more imagination. Perseus had only used it to reflect the image of the Gorgon. It had probably been cast away. Besides, I could barely manage the spear, let alone a heavy shield. What could I use that would do the same for me?

I had an idea. There was a camera on my mobile phone. It would be able to show me her image, so that I wouldn't have to look at her directly.

I charged it up, and sat back to wait for nightfall. If I struck before then she would still be in human form, and I would only hurt Emma. But if I killed the Gorgon, perhaps there was a slim chance I could save Emma. Unless I killed myself in the process.

I wrote a letter to my mother, explaining what I was about to do, and where the calcified bodies were. At first

I was going to hide it in my sister's bedroom, but she was so untidy I didn't think anyone would find it for weeks. So I left it behind the scales on the kitchen counter.

I checked my watch. As soon as night approached, I threw my mobile in my bag, dragged the spear, thumping and clanging, to the front door and set off. I would cut through the back streets and be at the Torrington Estate in just a few minutes.

This is nuts, I thought, closing the front door behind me. I made a pretty scruffy modern-day Perseus, armed with a mobile and a ridiculously long section of park railing. *I am so going to get wiped out.*

27: The Duel

I stood at the entrance to the Torrington Estate, the heavy spear leaning against my soaked body. The sun – if you could find it through the dense grey clouds – was preparing to steal away the light in less than twenty minutes.

This isn't like the old days, I told myself. *The hero doesn't always live, and it's going to get very nasty...*

I headed off across the quadrangle, towards the dark corner where the buildings met. Here the shadows crisscrossed in strange patterns. Cockroaches scuttled and rats made their nests in piles of wet trash.

I passed through the boiler room, into a scene from hell. Steam hissed from the riveted pipes that connected to the one working tank. The hot, moist air held something unhealthy and unpleasant. It smelled like stale, rotting old laundry. I stood in the doorway studying the room. I checked out the thick pile of rags where the creature came to sleep, the glistening scales it had shed on the floor, like bits of broken rainbow.

I walked further into the room, dragging the railing spear behind me. Flicking open my phone, I accessed the camera and turned it on. I studied the screen carefully, turning it first one way, then the other, scanning the room.

Behind me ran the central heating pipes to the apartments, stacks of ribbed steel tubing that coiled about one another in the overheated gloom. The pale light of my mobile shone across them, the miniature screen copying what I saw. I peered into the great pile of dirty rags, disturbing them with the tip of my spear. They kind of looked like a nest. I was really hoping not to find anything.

Silently, slowly, carefully, one pale greenish-brown pipe uncoiled itself behind me.

It took me a while to notice. I continued to dig into the rags, separating out torn scales, evidence of the Gorgon's occupation. The place smelled as musty as an animal's cage.

The pipe slowly dropped down, so slick, so silent. It was quickly followed by another. Something flickered on the screen of my mobile, and I turned.

The Gorgon had separated itself from the warm pipes, and was moving very slowly, inch by inch, towards me. I had seen a snake move like this on a TV programme, when it was advancing on a rat. And now I was the rat.

And then it was out of the shadows, and instead of a reptilian creature I saw it was still Emma. Her limbs were thinly covered in greenish grease that must have leaked from the pipes, and she was dressed in her demon T-shirt and scraps of rag she had taken from the nest. She looked at me with unseeing eyes, as if she was sleepwalking.

Then came a sound I had not heard before. Another hiss like steam escaping from the boiler, but becoming deeper, growing stronger every second, until it seemed to be coming from all around me. It was in my head, something that hadn't happened yet, something that was about to happen.

Emma let out a rumbling sigh that sounded a thousand years old. I'd forgotten about only looking in my mobile. I watched, transfixed, as she slowly started to change. I could tell that her human side was fading fast. In a few moments I knew she would only have animal instincts left. I had to get away from her.

Emma kept rubbing at her head. Now she started to moan. Several curls of fair hair came out between her fingers. Her skin grew pale as the blood drained from its surface. She scratched at her clothes, shredding her demon T-shirt into strips. I realized that her nails were growing with incredible speed. Her face and arms were covered in pointed scales. They divided and caught the light from the boiler reflecting an oily sheen.

She was clearly in pain now. Boil-sized bumps were

pushing themselves up on her skull. As each one burst, it released a tightly coiled green snake, sticky with body fluid, that grew like the tendrils of a fern. Her jaw lowered and stretched, the teeth thinning and lengthening.

Beneath the tingling fear what I felt most was a fascination for how all this was possible – her bones were actually changing their shape as the chemical balance of her body altered. After she had fed, when it was time to change back, the same chemical flow would work in reverse, dissolving the stone that had built up around her bones, leaving the original form there.

The oils that soaked her skin allowed it to stretch and change – the process was incredible, a science lesson going insanely wrong.

Her eyes had flattened out and turned a deep greenish-yellow. As she opened her mouth, I saw her tongue split in two and grow longer, until it flickered about her mouth, almost too long to coil in.

She was no longer Emma. The Gorgon was in full possession of her. The hissing grew deeper within her throat. The writhing mass of snakes on her head joined in the noise, as if they had been summoned. The ones that ran down the centre of her skull were the largest. At the base of her neck, the smallest were no bigger than wiggling green worms.

She stretched her throat and turned to stare at me.

'Look into my eyes. Look at me.'

I had become so fascinated with the transformation that I had neglected to keep watching in my phone. Suddenly it beeped in my hand – incredibly, I found myself looking at an incoming text message from my mother, demanding to know where I was. The sound was enough to make me remember the danger I was in. I watched on the screen as the fully transformed Gorgon darted straight for me. She moved with astonishing speed.

I fell back and dived for the space between the boilers. She hit the edge of a hot pipe and recoiled in an agonized burst of hisses. The steel plating had burned her shoulder.

I needed to reach the spear, but it was on the floor on the far side of the room. Scrambling over the wet concrete, I was able to grab the end, but it was heavy and the tipped point was caught behind a pipe.

I checked the mobile screen, tilting it around. Nothing. Where had she gone?

Suddenly the Gorgon flew at me. I saw glistening muscles propelling her body in my direction, but I saw the whole thing happening as if it was in slow motion. Raising my right foot, I lashed out and kicked at her stomach, sending her reeling back. She had fallen with her head away from me, lost in the shadows.

I needed to keep her at bay until I could free the spear. I could tell she was circling me, and would continue to move in closer, just as a snake would creep up on its prey.

I was lying on the floor, trying to lift the spear, but it was stuck fast.

Without thinking, I glanced back, too late to stop myself from the reflex action. She still hadn't moved, so I couldn't see her head. *Snakes are cunning*, I thought, *they stay still until the prey comes within range to strike.*

The camera screen of my mobile made her appear closer than she was. I knew I would have to take the difference into account. Remembering my backpack, I grabbed it and shook out the contents. The can of lighter fluid bounced onto the floor. Grabbing it, I flicked the top open and sprayed it across the concrete.

I checked the mobile screen; she was on the move, her limbs flexing and rising like snakes.

The lighter – in my pocket. I struck it against the pooling petrol and with a *whuumph* it flared in a blue streak across the room.

The Gorgon was halfway towards me when the fire flared up. She hissed and screamed at the sharp light, and fell back once more, but I knew that it wouldn't hold her. The flames were already starting to die down, and a few moments later they went out completely. The room had darkened.

I needed to free the spear. With difficulty I kept the mobile in my left hand, checking the screen.

The Gorgon lashed out with shocking speed, flicking her right arm toward me. She knocked the mobile from my hand. It slammed against the boiler, splitting open, its battery bouncing over the concrete.

Now I knew I wouldn't be able to find her again. I searched the room as much as I dared, but couldn't see her anywhere. The strange, deadening silence she carried around with her pressed against my eardrums like a warning alarm. I felt sick, blurred by the heat and the sound of blood pounding in my ears.

I needed something to fight back with. That was when I saw the garden rake leaning against the wall.

I knew she had to be right behind me. I grabbed the handle of the rake and swung it wide. The rake's prongs embedded themselves in her hair, and I pulled hard, tearing out a forkful of screaming snakes. I had gashed her neck. She retreated, dripping splashes of blood as she did so.

I watched as new snakes sprang up in the spilled blood, angry tangles of thin crimson worms that spiralled and rose like some mad chemistry experiment. I stamped on them before they could grow any bigger, but each new splash brought new nests of serpents.

I followed the writhing stains, crushing them out, slipping in the blood, expecting to confront the Gorgon at each step.

She had run to ground. A wave of thick silence passed through the room. There were a dozen places for her to hide. I ran back to the spear and kicked the end as hard as I could, so that the tip freed itself. Raising it up with some difficulty, I searched the boiler room, terrified that I might catch a glimpse of her face.

Nothing. Where the hell was she?

I checked the pieces of my mobile, but knew they couldn't be put back together. The case was broken. I leaned the spear against the wall and fell back, catching my breath. The pipes above me started to hiss and gurgle again as boiling water passed through them. I dared to look over at the tanks, trying to see where she had gone.

Silent as a snake. My own fault. I should have remembered.

She was standing just centimetres away from me, to one side. Motionless. Watching. Waiting. So close now that I could feel the ends of her split tongue wetly touching the side of my bare neck. I looked to her shadow thrown on the far wall, and saw the snakes on her head rising up as one, slowly arching, preparing to strike me at the exact same moment.

I knew this time there was no way out.

Without daring to look, I inched my arms upward to the overhead pipe and touched it. The hot metal seared my palms, but knew it was my only chance. With a sudden spring, I lifted myself off the floor and pulled down with all my might. The pipe burst open and emptied boiling water over her. Scalded, the snakes screamed and hissed, recoiling. I grabbed the spear and swung it up hard, piercing her clean through the shoulder. Hot blood sprayed over me from the wound.

I needed to kill the creature, but did not want Emma to die. I tried to remember – blood taken from which side of the Gorgon was lethal? Which side brought back life? Was it the left or the right?

I knew I'd have to take a guess; it was a fifty-fifty chance. I had punctured her right shoulder. Had I finished us both or saved us?

The spear jutted from her body. With a scream she fell down hard on her back, the spear-point jamming in the floor beneath her. I had to force myself to cover my eyes, knowing that otherwise I would look directly at her. Her right hand slapped the concrete floor rhythmically, as if seeking to attract my attention. I knew she was trying to force me to look. It was in her nature. *Look at me and meet your fate, this is my greatest weapon.*

But the Gorgon, pierced and pinned, was dying. The slapping hand grew slower and weaker. Her skin was already starting to turn grey. It was splitting and coming off in scaly sheets, like sunburned skin.

I dropped to my knees and tore the spear free, dragging it out of her flesh. The wound was large, and was bleeding badly. Would the Gorgon transform back, leaving Emma behind?

I felt sick and exhausted. I was pouring sweat. The air was overheated. I dropped the spear with a clang and collapsed on the floor, and the room went black. Heroes aren't supposed to faint.

28: Different Versions

When I came to, I found myself alone in the boiler room.

I tried to sit up too quickly, and was forced to lie down again because the room had started spinning. I slowly twisted my head and looked around. A few patches of blood, crushed snakes, nothing else to mark my battle with an ancient creature. Wincing, I raised myself onto one elbow and checked the room. It looked clear. More importantly, the normal sounds of the world had returned. It was suddenly cooler. The Gorgon had gone. She had vanished as quickly as she had appeared.

Rising and limping painfully outside, I followed a trail of blood speckles that led along the corridor, in the direction of the quadrangle. It was still dark, and raining lightly. Although the danger had passed, the world looked a more sinister place. The blood spots led from the path and disappeared into the patchy earth. Where was she?

Emma – the human, the real Emma – was lying on her back between tufts of grass, her eyes shut tight. She was smeared with blood and mud, and at first I thought she was dead. But then I checked her pulse, and found a faint but steady beat. The wound in her shoulder was dark with congealed gore, but was already turning into a normal human scab. She was covered in small cuts, probably the effect of the sudden change back.

I gently raised her head, and waited for her to regain consciousness. I waited, and waited. I don't know how long it took.

'Has she gone?'

I must have been dozing. Emma was awake and looking at me with a question on her face.

'I think so. She can't hurt us now. Reckon you can stand up?'

'Maybe, if you give me a hand. My shoulder.'

'I'm sorry about that.' I helped her to her feet. 'But it's over. You're safe. Lean on me.'

We hobbled out of the open quadrangle, heading to the colonnade that ran beneath the terraces of the flats. 'I know it was me,' she said flatly. 'I can remember everything. I attacked you.'

'It wasn't you, Emma. It was the virus. You didn't know who you were. I was just prey.'

'I caught it from the snakeskin. I think there were others who touched it before me and scratched themselves. Maybe they fought off the urge to kill until they finally died of starvation. Maybe I just wasn't strong enough.'

'You were very strong, Emma. For all we know there could be several infected Gorgons out there in different cities, who can tell? The Gorgon has walked before, and she dies if she doesn't feed. She has to kill to feed the hunger. That's why there are others who have disappeared. I thought the jar had been created to ward off evil, but instead it was used to bring evil here. Josun guarded it. Bet he didn't even know what it was, just kept everything in its place. What was it like – the infection?'

'Like a weird illness. At night my skin grew hard and scaly under the moon. I could pick little pieces off. At first Diane wanted to sit up with me, but I wouldn't let her. I was worried it might spread to her. I fell asleep, and while I slept I dreamed that I changed. I walked the streets trying to get rid of the pain inside me. But it was raining, and there was no one about. I could transform in the park and the basement because it was always dark there. The curse only works on females. That's why Gary was OK.'

'Do you remember what happened to him?'

'One night Gary was waiting for me, worried. He'd found my bedroom empty. By now I knew that if I looked at him, his skin would rot and become crusted and turn as hard as stone, and he would die.'

'So you avoided looking at him?'

'Yes, but the snakes wanted to feed on his blood. I hung onto him tightly, making sure he couldn't look into my eyes. But the craving overtook me, and I wrapped myself around him tightly, tighter, until I could hear myself popping his bones from their sockets. First his arms, then his legs. And I kept tightening my grip until I could hear his spine splinter and crack. His eyes rolled up in his head and I knew he was dead.'

'You took him somewhere?'

'To the boiler room. I burned his remains in the furnace.' She raised a thin arm. 'It made me strong, you see. It's hard to explain what it was like. It took away pity and fear and sadness. And when I awoke the next morning, I was normal again, with no memory of what had happened. It was like that for a while, like the virus was asleep inside me.'

'That's because you were following the cycle of the moon.'

'But it was still growing in me. There were dreams of walking the streets and searching. And some secret part of me knew that the dreams were real. I would go to the gates of Viper's Green. I was drawn there. But I couldn't get back in. I couldn't find Gary's keys. Then I found that you and Max had cut open the lock. So I went inside. I made my way to the crypt, to see where I had come from.'

We didn't let the Gorgon out, I realized with a jolt. *Max's father did that when he took the skin. But we allowed it to get back in.*

'I kept the bodies there, where so many snakes had lived and died. I really didn't want to hurt anyone – but it wasn't me, you see. The Gorgon took over. I saw you and followed you – you felt me walking behind you. I know now that I was two people inside. Like it was more than just a bunch of germs. The spirit of the Gorgon wanted to take revenge against all the men of the world. I didn't know if I was inside her or she was inside me. My body would have grown exhausted from the changes, and I suppose she would have infected someone else and started all over again. And so it would continue. Each time she changed, a small part of me died. I don't think I could have survived another night.'

'But it's over,' I told her gently. 'You're alive.'

'Yes, I'm alive, but there's something—' She stopped.

'What's the matter?'

'Medusa – the Gorgon. I thought the only way to kill her was to cut off her head.'

'No, I couldn't do that. I'd have killed you. I used the spear that Sir Richard Torrington brought back from Libya. He hid it in the railings of Viper's Green. A safety precaution for anyone who could work it out.'

'I don't understand. I thought Perseus used the spear to pin her down and then cut off her head with his sword. I'm sure of it. He took the head away with him, and its gaze was still deadly – even after its head had been cut off the Gorgon could turn people to stone.'

'I don't know,' I replied wearily. 'There are many different versions of the story.'

'But she was inside me – she took something from every person she killed to make her stronger.'

I had a terrible thought. 'I'm an idiot,' I told her. 'There's something I've completely overlooked. The snakeskin. It must still be around here somewhere.'

'You're right. Whenever I'm near it I can transform. I think eventually the Gorgon will be powerful enough to change without a body.'

'She's building up her strength until she can fill the snakeskin out by—'

I didn't get a chance to finish the sentence. We both noticed it at the same time; the sounds of the city had suddenly died away. They were replaced by a new noise, a deep rattling hiss, the deepest yet, larger and more terrifying than anything we had heard before.

Snakes were meant to shed their skins. This one had become so strong she could finally do it in reverse. She no longer needed a host.

From the darkness of the open corridor an immense green serpent uncoiled and rose up before us, glittering with emerald scales, marked with a familiar zigzag viper pattern down its back.

We ran for the quadrangle, but the snake was faster.

29: The Great Snake

The immense reptile arched a full three metres into the air, its wide triangular head angled down, flat vertical yellow eyes staring. Its black tongue flickered out at me between long hinged fangs. Its jaw could open one hundred and eighty degrees. Its venom was lethal. It was wholly reptile. No human part remained.

It was the worst thing that could possibly have happened. The creature had successfully separated from its host. It had gained enough genetic material from its human victims to exist without them. It was no longer reliant on mere humans for survival.

Emma froze in shock. Neither of us could look away. The great snake coiled higher, higher, mesmerizing us. It took a moment to choose its victim – but then, swiftly and silently, it struck.

Sweeping down with great red jaws slowly opening, it clamped them around my upper arm and bit down hard, the muscles in its jaws fattening as it injected its venom into my body. For what seemed like an age, it held its tight grip.

The searing, numbing pain flooded my arm, then my shoulder, my neck. I could feel the venom pouring in. Oddly it was ice cold, spreading through my veins like melting snow. The great snake's jaw clamped ever tighter, cutting off my blood supply.

Finally, it pulled free and released me, its poison spent. I fell to the ground in surprise, a cry dying in my throat, my hands rising to the terrible wound. The pain was incredible. Once, I had shut my fingers in the hinge-side of my bedroom door and my nails had turned black – this was the same kind of pain, but all over. The corridor started to telescope away and fade. I was filled with fire and ice.

The snake coiled itself high once more and turned to its remaining victim, preparing to strike again. Emma had backed up against the wall of the corridor. There was nowhere to go. I realized I had fallen onto the ground beside her. The wound on my arm was hardening fast and spreading.

It's over, I thought. *This is how the myth really ends. With the triumph of the beast.*

I saw, but didn't fully register what happened next. Operating on her natural reflexes, without even stopping to think, Emma picked up the battered gardener's shovel that leaned against the wall, the one that had stood there for so long that no one even noticed it any more.

Her fingers tightened around the handle and she swung it as hard as she could manage.

The blade swept down. It bit deep into the great snake's neck. Caught by surprise, the serpent fell over onto its side, its head hitting the concrete. But when Emma tried to get close, the tail lashed out at her, knocking her back. She fell hard.

But it could not dislodge the shovel from its neck. Thrashing back and forth, it released a roar that shook my bones. Emma ran to its screaming head and kicked down hard on the blade of the shovel, as if she was digging earth.

She leaned on it with all her weight, sawing the edge through the snake's muscular flesh until she felt its vertebrae pop open. Still she kept up the pressure, pushing down harder and harder, forcing the spade through the gory pale meat of its body. It was all muscle, tough and strong – but no match for sharp steel.

Spattered with blood, I dimly heard her scream into the sky as she pushed down.

Finally, the head was cut through and rolled away, perfectly severed. The stump pumped a great geyser of blood into the earth, emptying its poison sacs, reeking and steaming.

No new snakes grew there. The creature, in its final reptilian form, was dying.

But so was I. Emma knelt down and checked my eyes. I knew I had no more than a few moments left to live.

She did the only thing she could think of doing. Moving to the pouring neck of the beast, she caught the cascading blood in her cupped hands and leaked it over my bite wound. Her actions were instinctive. Having become a part of the Gorgon's myth, she knew that its life force contained both venom and antidote.

I hallucinated. I saw unimaginable horrors. Images tumbled through my head like a cascade of all my worst nightmares put together.

The poison had taken hold in me, but the cure was far more powerful. Cupping the fresh blood in endless handfuls, she emptied it onto me. She told me later that it took over an hour to take effect, but eventually I started to revive. And something was happening to the great snake; the meat was degrading, rotting into the earth, putrefying, leaving behind only its shed skin. The patterned scales were already drying and returning to their old form – the skin of the Gorgon.

'We did it,' she whispered, lying back on the earth, exhausted.

Emma and I should have yelled our triumph into the night air, but we couldn't find the power to do so. We had lost Max, and so many others had died. Emma lay beside me in the falling rain, and I knew I would live and be well. I felt sure that our friendship, forged in blood, would outlast any legend.

Although I couldn't help wondering what on earth would happen to the Gorgon's skin this time.

30: Snakes Alive

When we had recovered a bit, we knew we had to go back to Viper's Green one more time. Emma thought we should bury Max in the graveyard where the whole thing had started, but I thought we should take him back to Jackie, even if it meant getting into a mess with the cops. As it turned out, it didn't make any difference what either of us thought, because when we got to the spot where Max fell we found nothing except a big patch of flattened grass.

'Where is he?' she asked.

'That's weird.' I figured the Gorgon had dragged his body away and put it somewhere. We looked all around the place, but still couldn't find it.

Mystified, I went home and hastily swiped back my letter of explanation before Mum and Lucy could read it. Not that it had even been moved; nobody shifts things to clean in our house.

'Alfie Jai Hellion, is that you?' my mother called, and I knew I was in trouble. 'Come in here, I've hardly seen you in days.'

I stopped on the stairs. 'I've got stuff to do, can it wait?'

'Nice try. You don't have to do your homework right now. I'm making a curry.'

'You're always making a curry.'

Reluctantly, I came back downstairs and went into the kitchen. My mother was stirring crimson strands of meat in bubbling sauce. They swirled back and forth, making me feel sick. My mother dried her hands and gave me a hug. 'I never see you these days. You're always out. Don't grow up too fast, Red. Try to enjoy the time.'

'Fine, OK, I'm not a child, can you let me go now?' I pulled myself free.

Lucy was in the lounge, scrunched up on the sofa. She was threading fat bits of cotton wool between her toes to allow her nail polish to dry. 'Ask it where it's been,' she called out to our mother.

I walked over and stood in front of her. Lucy's hair was filled with bright green bendy curlers. She looked like a comedy version of the Gorgon.

'Hey, get out of the way, Creature, I'm trying to watch *Strictly Come Dancing*.'

I reached back and turned off the television. 'You're not to call me The Creature any more, Lucy. And if you have something to say to me, say it to my face. Don't go through Mum like a coward.'

'Mum, stop it from talking to me like this!' She waved me away with freshly varnished pink nails. She prided herself on being the pinkest girl in the neighbourhood.

I leaned in closer. 'I'm not an *It*, I'm a *He*. If you don't start respecting me, I'll tell everyone where you really go at night.'

'You don't know where I go. What do you know about girls?'

'I know everything about you, Lucy. You have no secrets from me. Here's a tip: if you keep a diary with a lock on it, don't store the key in the same drawer.'

'You have no right to go through my stuff!'

'And you shouldn't be seeing someone who's twenty-two and dating someone else.'

'So the worm has finally turned,' Lucy hissed back in shock. 'What's got into you? When did you get so tough?'

'I'm not a worm, either. A mere worm wouldn't be able to kill a poisonous snake.' I walked away from my mystified sister and headed for my bedroom.

I slept for a full ten hours. But when I awoke, I began to wonder if things could ever go back to normal without knowing what happened to Max. Then later that morning, something *really* weird happened.

I got a text. It said: 'I'm in the Royal Free Hospital. Bring some decent food. Max.'

We couldn't believe it. He'd been given an actual room of his own, and he looked terrible. His upper body was covered in huge blue-black blotches, but at least he was sitting up in bed, alive.

'What the hell happened?' I asked. 'I saw you get bitten over and over again.'

'The doctor reckons I had an allergic reaction, but there wasn't any poison in the bites,' he croaked. 'These are bruises. I've had loads of tests but they can't find any venom left in my system.'

I knew why. The Gorgon had been driven to strike by its nature, but part of her — the Emma part — was desperate not to kill him, even though she didn't realize it. That was why she hadn't looked him in the eye — instead of turning him to stone, she had attacked him and left him for dead, but had managed to hold back the venom and spare his life.

'Oh yeh, and thanks for making sure I was OK,' said Max. 'Some friend you turned out to be. What did you bring me to eat?'

'Grapes and a Mars bar,' I said, still stunned.

'Is that it? I was hoping you'd smuggle in some KFC. You're a rubbish hospital visitor.'

'We can get you some,' I said, and Emma nodded happily. We were both so glad to see him that we'd have done anything he suggested right then.

'Man, that's nasty,' said Max, pointing to Emma's shoulder. 'What happened to you?'

'He did it.' Emma pointed at me.

'I didn't want to hurt her,' I explained. 'I did as little damage as possible.'

'Well that's something, I guess.'

'How did you get here?' I wanted to know.

'I woke up and it was freezing, and tried to walk home but I couldn't manage it. I got hit by a car right outside the park. Just a bump, but the driver brought me here.' He looked at me, then at Emma. 'So, what's been going on with you two?'

We tried to explain what had happened, but each time we started over, it just sounded crazier and crazier.

Finally I said, 'I'll tell you what I think really happened. We found a dirty old snakeskin and we got water from the crypt on us. We picked up some kind of weird germ. And it gave us violent hallucinations. We tried to make sense of what we'd seen, and came up with this mad story. We've got no proof it ever happened.'

'My mother knows,' said Emma.

'Your mum's barking mad,' said Max, shovelling in the rest of the Mars bar.

'Then how do you explain the disappearances, and what happened to that guy in the grocery store, and the old drunk, Gabriel? And Josun?' Emma asked. 'They're all missing.'

'I don't know,' I admitted. 'Maybe Gabriel and Josun really did die. Maybe something really did happen to

Nalin. Or maybe we just thought it did. People move away, or die or disappear all the time.'

'Well, I don't buy it,' said Max.

'Neither do I,' Emma agreed. 'We didn't just imagine it.'

'So, who are we going to tell?'

'No one.'

'No one.'

'Exactly.'

We shook on it. Three hands together.

31: Blood Ties

Max had to stay in for observation, and I got three days off school and a stupid tetanus jab at the hospital. I'd told everyone I'd had a fight with a mad Alsatian, and that it had bitten me before I'd managed to lay it out, not exactly the truth. But even the thicko-bullies in my class started looking at me with a weird new kind of respect. I liked that.

Mum was just annoyed. She said, 'We should change your family name from Hellion, because that's what it looks like I've raised. I always thought you were going to be the bookish, quiet one.'

I looked up 'Hellion'. It means 'troublesome, rowdy, disorderly, mischievous – a hell-raiser'. Cool. But weird how she never mentioned that before. I guess she hadn't wanted to give me ideas.

I thought about the strange visions I'd had, this other part of my brain that had opened up like an extra sense. I wondered if it would ever happen again. I was going to confide in Emma, but didn't find the courage – funny, considering all we'd been through.

Three months later, the last two families were moved from the Torrington Estate to new houses nearby. Emma, Max and I promised to stay in touch. We had to – we were bound by ties of blood. But I think we were all a bit different after that, like we'd somehow shed our own skins and grown. We argued a lot about what really happened in Viper's Green, and never really managed to sort it out. The main thing was that the three of us, Emma, Max and me, had each other. It was a friendship that would never be broken.

A few weeks after that, the first builders and bright yellow bulldozers turned up. I went over to watch as they started to tear apart the wet turf of the estate's quadrangle. After a few minutes, one of the workmen called his mates over to look at the wet reddish-coloured hole they had dug.

'What's the matter?' said his mate, peering into the ragged clay pit.

'I thought I saw something.'

'What sorta something? I don't see nothing.'

I craned forward, trying to see for myself, but didn't want them to catch me looking.

'I swear, when we lifted out the earth the ground was full of snakes, really thin ones, white and green they were.'

'Well, where are they now?'

The workman scratched his chin, puzzled. 'I don't know. Honest. There was hundreds of 'em. Maybe they don't like the light.'

'Reckon you imagined it,' said his mate. 'We're digging this lot out, so if there's anything inside the ground, it will have to find somewhere else to live. There's tunnels under here, you know, part of the Tube line. If they've gone down onto the platforms, they ain't half going to give the passengers a fright.' He cast one look back at the hole, but saw nothing. 'Come on,' he said, 'let's get back to work. I want to get home early. The wife's cooking my favourite tonight.'

'What's that?'

'Spaghetti Bolognese.'

Whatever had been exposed to daylight was now burrowing fast and deep, searching for human warmth. It was time for me to go.

HACKING TIMBUKTU

STEPHEN DAVIES

Long ago in the ancient city of Timbuktu a student pulled off the most daring heist in African history – the theft of 100 million pounds worth of gold. It was never recovered but now a cryptic map of its whereabouts has been discovered.

Danny Temple is a good traceur and a great computer hacker. When the map falls into his hands and he finds himself pursued by a bizarre group calling itself *The Knights of Akonio Dolo*, both of these skills are tested to the limit. From the streets of London to the sands of Timbuktu, this high-tech gold rush does not let up for a moment.

9781842708842   £5.99

THE
TRAP

JOHN SMELCER

Johnny pulled the fur-lined hood of his parka over his head and walked towards his own cabin with the sound of snow crunching beneath his boots.
'He should be back tomorrow,' he thought.

Johnny's grandfather is out checking trap lines, but he has been gone much too long. Proud, stubborn and determined to be independent he may be, but he has caught a foot in his own trap and hasn't the strength to free himself. As Johnny worries about him, he is menaced by wolves, plummeting temperatures and hunger. Does he have enough wilderness craft and survival instinct to stay alive? Will Johnny find him in time?

'An unforgettable story. Brilliant!' Ray Bradbury

9781842707395 £5.99